"Listen, Trent. About last night . . ."

"Yeah. I wanted to talk to you about that too," he said, his voice growing more serious. "What do you say we meet up at House of Java after school some-time?"

"Well . . ." Tia hesitated, absently coiling a long lock of hair around her index finger.

She should say no. She should explain about Angel. But he sounded so enthusiastic, so *into* her—unlike Angel, who couldn't even pick up his phone.

"Come on," he urged. "I want to make sure you're real and not some beautiful vision I imagined."

Tia laughed. Beautiful vision? How many times had he used *that* line? *And how many times has it worked?* Tia wondered, staring at her reddening re-flection in her full-length mirror. *Don't fall for it, Tee,* she told herself. *This is just your hormones talking. Don't be an idiot.* But somehow her inner voice didn't sound all that convincing.

"Tia? You might as well say yes because I'm not going to hang up until you do," Trent said.

"All right," Tia heard herself say. "How about we meet Wednesday around five-thirty?"

Don't miss any of the books in SWEET VALLEY HIGH
SENIOR YEAR, an exciting series from Bantam Books!

Visit the Official Sweet Valley Web Site on the Internet at:

http://www.sweetvalley.com

Francine Pascal's **senioryear**

SVH

Split Decision

CREATED BY
FRANCINE PASCAL

BANTAM BOOKS
NEW YORK • TORONTO • LONDON • SYDNEY • AUCKLAND

RL: 6, AGES 012 AND UP

SPLIT DECISION
A Bantam Book / February 2000

Sweet Valley High® is a registered trademark of Francine Pascal.
Conceived by Francine Pascal.
Cover photography by Michael Segal.

Produced by 17th Street Productions, Inc.
33 West 17th Street
New York, NY 10011.

ISBN: 0-553-49313-2

Visit us on the Web! www.randomhouse.com/teens

Published simultaneously in the United States and Canada

Bantam Books is an imprint of Random House Children's Books, a
division of Random House, Inc. BANTAM BOOKS and the rooster
colophon are registered trademarks of Random House, Inc. Bantam Books,
1540 Broadway, New York, New York 10036.

PRINTED IN THE UNITED STATES OF AMERICA

OPM   0 9 8 7 6 5 4 3 2 1

To Laurie Wenk

melissa Fox

I've heard all those warm, fuzzy sayings about how it doesn't matter whether you win or lose, blah, blah, blah. Or that winning isn't everything. Or all that "do-unto-others" stuff. The fact is, the people who wrote all that crap were losers. I mean, let's face it. Winning matters. You've got to know what you want and go after it. And if you don't get it, you're a loser—no matter how many feel-good quotes you hide behind.

I like to win. I really, really do. And you want to know one of the best things about getting what I want? Making losers out of the people I take it from.

Will Simmons

I know what some people are going to say—that I'm whipped. That I'm a wuss. That all Melissa has to do is snap her fingers . . .

Personally I think it takes a bigger man to admit he did the wrong thing and to go back if that's what's really good for him.

Besides, it's not really <u>going back.</u> Things are going to be different this time.

I'm sure of it.

Trent Maynor

To: jaames@cal.rr.com
From: trent#1@cal.rr.com
Re: Those crazy SVH girls

Hey, Aames! I met the coolest girl last night at the party. Her name is Tia. She and I hit it off well. I mean _really_ well. Unfortunately she had to leave just when things were getting going, and I didn't have a chance to get her number or anything. All I know is she's a cheerleader at SVH, which means she must know Jessica, which means you might know her. Give me the details!

Jeremy Aames

To: trent#1@cal.rr.com
From: jaames@cal.rr.com
Re: re: Those crazy SVH girls

   Yeah, I know her. She's cool. I
know she had a serious boyfriend for
a long time. But don't sweat it. The
guy left for college, so they must
have ended things beforehand. Tia
doesn't seem like the type to mess
around behind a guy's back.

Conner McDermott

Tia once told me that if Angel hooked up behind her back, she'd break up with him instantly.

I never knew my best friend was a hypocrite.

Tia rolled over in bed and opened her eyes. Sunshine was streaming through her bedroom window, and a bird sang softly from the tree outside. A storybook morning. She smiled, stretched her arms, and sat up.

A ray of light was illuminating something on her desk. It was the silvery oval frame that held Angel's senior portrait. Something about the way the sunlight hit it made it almost glow.

Suddenly a distant thought started to come into focus, as if the clouds of her mind were parting. Angel. Hadn't called. Party. Another guy. Trent . . . ? She and Trent kissing in the corner . . .

"Oh God!" Tia whispered, bringing her hands to her temples. Had she actually made out with some other guy at the party last night?

A heavy sensation sank down into her gut. There were words for people like her. *Cheater. Slut. Back-stabber.* That was what Elizabeth had called herself when she was fooling around with Conner behind Maria's back.

Elizabeth . . . and Conner.

1

The heavy sensation grew even heavier and the clouds in her mind lifted completely as another memory revealed itself: Elizabeth and Conner's shocked expressions as she and that Trent guy walked into the bedroom. Great. What must they think of her? Angel was their friend, and he was out of town for about five seconds before Tia was messing around behind his back. Tia hurriedly pulled on a pair of jeans and a T-shirt and headed for her door. As soon as she opened it, she found her brother Miguel standing in the hall.

"Oh. You're up. Finally," he said. "Conner's here."

Conner stepped into the doorway behind Miguel. His expression was made of stone. His brown hair stuck up slightly on one side, and his green eyes looked droopier than usual. Had he raced right out of bed to come over and confront her?

"Thanks, Migs," she mumbled. "You can go now."

Miguel rolled his eyes and loped off down the hallway.

Tia tried to meet Conner's eyes, but something—guilt, perhaps?—kept pulling her head down. "Come on in," she said, straightening her pink T-shirt.

Conner stepped through the doorway to the center of the room. But instead of flopping down on her bed or straddling her desk chair in his usual manner, he just stood there, watching her.

"You're up early," she remarked as lightly as possible.

Conner didn't even crack a smile. "Tia, what the hell happened last night?"

Tia sighed and sat on her bed. "I don't know," she mumbled.

"What do you mean, you don't know?" he asked, an unfamiliar edge to his voice. "Angel's been gone for what, ten seconds?"

Amazing how Conner always knew exactly what she was thinking—practically to the letter.

"Tee?"

"I know!" she blurted out, jumping to her feet and pushing her hands through her dark, sleep-tangled hair. "I'm the worst person ever to walk the face of the planet. But it was just that . . . Well, Angel hasn't returned any of my phone calls or e-mails in like five days. Then I finally called and got ahold of him before the party last night and he sounded so . . . distant. There were all these voices in the background—"

"What? Girls?" Conner let out an exasperated grunt. "Tee, you know Angel would never—"

"No! Guys *and* girls. What I'm saying is . . . is that it made me feel like . . ." She paused. Her voice was shaking slightly, and she hated when that happened.

"Like what?" Conner asked, crossing his arms over the front of his green T-shirt.

Tia took a deep breath. "Like . . . this sounds so stupid, but it's like I'm not part of his world anymore," she said quickly, her heart responding with a pang as she heard herself say the words out loud. She

3

sank back down onto the bed and shut her eyes, trying to dam up the tide of emotions.

Conner remained silent for several long seconds. Then he exhaled heavily and sat down beside her. He pushed her hair back from her face, and Tia half smiled. "Look, if you're scared Angel is shutting you out . . . then deal with it. But I know you, Tee. And breaking in a new groping partner is just going to make you feel worse."

Tia snorted a laugh. Conner had such a way with bluntness.

"I know you're right," Tia said, staring down at her hands. "I guess part of me . . . I thought I was sort of getting back at Angel, you know? Stupid, huh?"

"I've hooked up for a lot worse reasons," Conner said. He rubbed his hand across his forehead, and Tia knew he was choosing his words carefully. "It's not like I think I should be preaching to you," he said finally. "It's just you and Angel both deserve better. Don't mess it up."

Conner ran his hand through his dark, spiky hair and stared out the window. Tia suddenly realized how lucky she was to have a best friend who would roll out of bed on a Sunday morning and come talk through her problems with her.

"Hey," Tia said, reaching out and squeezing Conner's shoulder. He turned his head and looked her directly in the eyes. "Can I have a hug?" Tia asked.

Conner shook his head at her silliness but

smiled. He reached over and caught her up in a casual hug. Tia closed her eyes and squeezed back tightly. "Thanks, Conner."

"You okay?" Conner asked, releasing her and standing up.

"Yeah." Tia shrugged and tried to look normal. She was still completely confused, but she knew Conner had had his fill of emotional baggage for about a month, let alone one morning. "You know me," she said with a smile. "Bounce-back Tia."

Too bad she didn't believe it.

Andy Marsden fired several rounds from his X-wing fighter's laser guns, nuked the correct pathway, and flew to safety before the Death Star exploded into tiny bits.

"Yes!" he exclaimed, raising a fist in the air. "Nothing but shrapnel! Once again I have saved humanity from the dark forces of evil! Now I alone can rule the universe—ha, ha, ha, ha!"

"Excuse me? Mr. Jedi Knight?" Andy looked up to find his mother standing in the doorway of his room. "Now that you've completed your mission, could I talk to you for a moment?"

A sheepish grin stretched across Andy's freckled face. He set down the game controls. "Sure, Mom. What's up?"

Mrs. Marsden slowly stepped into the room. She stared at Andy for a second, frowned, opened her mouth to say something, and then turned and wandered over to his bookshelf.

"Y'all right, there, Mom?" Andy asked, pushing his curly red hair off his forehead.

"I'm fine," she said. "So, how was the party last night?" She picked up a comic book and absently flipped through it.

"Uh . . . fine?" he replied. What was with the fidgety act?

"And how are things at school?" she asked over her shoulder as she inspected the *South Park* poster on the wall above his bed.

"Okay," he said.

"Andy, do you have anything you want to tell me? Anything important?" she asked.

Andy's mind zoomed. Uh-oh. What happened? Did his brother rat on him about breaking her antique vase during their last impromptu wrestling match, the one she assumed the cat had knocked over? Or could she actually be leading into one of those "safe-sex-and-you" conversations? Fab.

"Uh . . . not really, Mom," he said as his leg started to bounce. "Everything's fine."

"Then what's this?" His mother handed him a pink slip of paper. "I found it in the hallway. It must have fallen out of your backpack."

Andy studied the paper and sighed in relief. It was the notice he got in class last week telling him to report to the counselor's office. "It's nothing, Mom.

Mr. Nelson just wanted to talk about my plans for college and stuff. That's all."

His mother raised her eyebrows. "Are you sure? You didn't switch the boys' and girls' rest-room signs again, did you? Or fake an anxiety attack to get out of gym?"

"No, no." Andy shook his head. "Really, Mom. All the seniors are meeting with the counselors to discuss postgraduation plans. I swear."

She studied his face for a few heartbeats before relaxing. "All right, then," she said, walking over to his bed and perching on the one nonrumpled corner. "So tell me, what *are* your big plans for after school?"

He shrugged. "Oh, you know. First I have to train with Master Yoda for a few years or so. Then I need to find a good right-hand man or couple of robots that can help me out. Plus there's the whole business of finding my lost twin sister and all . . ."

"Forget I asked." His mother shook her head and walked out the door.

"Don't worry, Mom," he called after her. "I won't go over to the dark side! No matter how much money they promise me!"

Andy smiled to himself. *That was close!* he thought. *This calls for another game.* He reached down to pick up the controls and noticed the pink note from the counselor's office lying next to the controls.

Oh, yeah. *That.* He'd promised Mr. Nelson last week that he'd join some sort of club, but he was still completely clueless about which one. It wasn't like they had anything really cool at Sweet Valley. Like a laser-tag team or a study group for the *X-Files* conspiracy theorists.

He knew he had to do something, though. And soon. If he wanted any chance at college, he had to prove himself a well-rounded, involved student citizen. Even if it meant signing up for something lame.

Tia sat on her bed, staring down at the framed portrait of Angel in her hands. Funny. She'd always thought his smile was wider than that. And that his eyes drooped more at the corners. Had she forgotten what he looked like already? Or was it that the photo simply didn't do justice to the live, in-the-flesh version of him?

"Give it back! Give it back! It's mi-ine!" Tomás's voice sliced through the wall and pierced Tia's brain like a Ginsu knife. Time for her brothers' daily battle over the Game Boy. Tia lay down on the bed and placed a pillow over her exposed ear, never taking her eyes off Angel.

Should she tell him about what happened at the party? Maybe confessing the whole thing to him would ease her conscience. At the very least she needed to open up about how left out she'd been feeling.

"No fair! I was playing this first!"

"But it's mine!"

"You weren't even here. You were downstairs watching TV!"

"I don't care! It's mine! Give it back!"

"All right. That's it," Tia muttered. She leaped off the bed and ran next door to her brothers' room.

8

"How much sugar did you guys eat today?" she hollered from the doorway. "Do you even *know* how to be quiet? Or do you just think you're the only ones on this block with eardrums!"

Tomás and Miguel froze in midargument, their dark brown eyes wide as golf balls. Just then Tia's mother rounded the corner of the hallway and frowned at all three of them.

"Boys, no more fighting," she ordered. "I want you two to go downstairs and settle this quietly." The boys mutely obeyed. As soon as they trudged past, Mrs. Ramirez turned toward Tia and laid a hand on her shoulder. "Well, that outburst wasn't like you, Tia. What's wrong?"

Tia raked her fingers into her thick brown hair, grasping her forehead tightly. A sharp pain was throbbing inside her skull. "Nothing," she said. Her mother wasn't exactly the type of person who would understand random party hookups. Tia was pretty sure her mom thought she and Angel were still in the peck-on-the-cheek phase.

"Are you sure?" her mother asked.

"Yes," Tia said evenly. Then she closed her eyes and took in a deep breath. "I just need to be left alone for a minute. Would it be all right if I borrowed the van? I need to sit somewhere quiet and think for a while."

Her mother nodded slowly, wiping her hands on the dish towel she seemed to almost constantly be carrying. "All right. But don't be out too long, okay?"

"Okay."

Tia headed into the hall and grabbed the keys from their usual spot on the table by the door. Free at last! It was just too impossible to have a productive train of thought in this house.

She started up the minivan and let it roar loudly. Then she backed out of the driveway and headed down the street.

The quiet hum of the engine helped her relax, and the brilliant sunshine seemed to be illuminating everything just for her. Tia turned onto the main strip, easily blending into the sparse Sunday traffic.

Sunday. When Angel was here, they'd often meet up at House of Java and talk about the weekend's events. There was nothing more cozy and comfortable than drowning in Angel's eyes . . . and a huge cup of latte. Tia hadn't even realized she was driving toward HOJ until it loomed into view. Some habits must die hard.

No sense stopping, though. She didn't feel like having coffee alone, and being there would only make her feel more miserable. Instead she should find someplace that didn't remind her of Angel.

But where? As she headed down the avenue, every single place held some sort of memory for her. The restaurants. The movie theater. The ice cream parlor and minigolf course. After three years of dating, there was really no place they hadn't visited at least once together.

Without thinking, she rounded a corner and drove down several blocks before turning onto a tree-lined street—a street as familiar to her as her own. Angel's street.

Tia parked the van across the road from his house. For a long moment she sat staring at his bedroom. Fragments of memories flashed past her, like a vivid parade of time. Angel laughing. Angel stroking her hair. Angel surprising her with flowers.

"God, what's wrong with me?" she cried, the van's cramped interior absorbing the sound of her voice.

How could she have even *considered* being with someone else? After everything she and Angel had been through and meant to each other? What did that say about her? About *them?*

Covering her face with her hands, Tia slumped over the steering wheel and cried. She felt beyond guilty. And the thing was, Angel was probably the only person in the world who could lift her spirits.

Maybe she should just go back home and call him. Then again, he knew her so well, he'd probably be able to tell something awful was up just by the sound of her voice. Should she risk it?

Tia straightened up and restarted the engine. In any case, she probably should head back. The drive wasn't exactly making her feel better.

After one last look at Angel's house, she pulled away from the curb and headed off. In a way, it seemed fitting she should be driving around aimlessly. Since Angel left, all she seemed to be doing was going around in circles.

Jessica Wakefield

<u>Perfect</u> is a word that gets a lot of abuse. You can find the <u>perfect</u> outfit for a party or have <u>perfect</u> weather for a trip to the beach. But attaching the adjective to a person can be dangerous.

In spite of all the daydreams, no one person is going to be just perfect for anyone else. At this point I know that better than anyone.

Will isn't the perfect guy. But I'm not a perfect girl either. So maybe we could both change in the right ways and, after a while, try to <u>perfect</u> our relationship. Maybe that's as close as it gets.

People should forget <u>perfect</u> as an adjective. <u>Perfect</u> as a verb is much more doable.

CHAPTER 2
Going Back

Tia parked the van in the driveway and took a deep breath before heading back into the house. Her long drive might have helped her sort things out, but it didn't ease her mood much. Hopefully she could avoid the rest of her family for a while and drown her sorrows with a package of chocolate-chip cookies.

She walked through the front door and was on a direct path to the kitchen when Jesse suddenly appeared at the entrance to the dining room.

"Hey. There you are," he said. He didn't even look up from the Game Boy he was abusing with his thumbs.

Tia rolled her eyes. With five kids *privacy* was not a word in the Ramirez dictionary. At least Ricky was away at college.

"Not now, Jesse. I need to get a snack." She side-stepped around him and resumed her trajectory toward the cookie jar.

"You just got a phone call. I told him you were still out, though. I didn't hear you come back."

Tia froze. Did he say phone call? Told *him*? It figured

that the one time she was out of the house, she'd missed Angel's call.

"He wanted you to call him back," Jesse continued, staring at the tiny screen. "Some guy named Trent. His number's on the table."

Tia's stomach tightened as she glanced down and snatched up the paper. *Trent* called? How did he get her number?

"Thanks, Jesse," she said quietly as she turned and headed toward her room.

"Hey! I thought you were gonna eat."

"I changed my mind," she called over her shoulder. Her chocolate craving was gone—probably a result of the instantaneous nausea she was suffering. Just when she thought she had everything figured out, he had to call. She hadn't counted on ever seeing or hearing from Trent again. She hadn't even given him her full name. Was the guy psychic or what?

Tia wadded up the paper into a tidy ball, but just as she was about to launch it into her garbage can, something stopped her.

Why shouldn't she call him? She and Trent had only hung out for one night and he'd called her right away—unlike a certain other person she knew who couldn't pick up a phone. She loved Angel, but that still didn't change the fact that this noncommunication stung. If Trent was going to be this polite, the least she could do was level with the guy.

Tia picked up her phone and dialed Trent's number. Her heart skipped from nervousness when she heard the click of the line being answered.

"Hello?"

"Uh . . . is this Trent?" Tia asked.

"Guilty."

"Hi, this is Tia."

"Oh, hey!" Trent said. "I'm glad you called."

"Yeah. Um, how did you get my number?" Tia asked, turning the paper over and over in her hand. Why was she so jittery?

"I hope you don't mind the detective work," Trent said with a chuckle. "After I lost you last night, I got your last name from a friend and tried four different Ramirezes in the book before I reached your place."

Tia smiled. It was flattering to think she'd made such a big impression. But she shouldn't let that get to her. She had to level with him about Angel. Right now.

"Listen, Trent. About last night . . ."

"Yeah. I wanted to talk to you about that too," he said, his voice growing more serious. "What do you say we meet up at House of Java after school sometime?"

"Well . . ." Tia hesitated, absently coiling a long lock of hair around her index finger.

She should say no. She should explain about Angel, hang up, and never see or hear from Trent again. But he sounded so enthusiastic, so *into* her—unlike Angel, who couldn't even pick up his phone.

"Come on," he urged. "I want to make sure you're

real and not some beautiful vision I imagined."

Tia laughed. Beautiful vision? How many times had he used *that* line? *And how many times has it worked?* Tia wondered, staring at her reddening reflection in her full-length mirror.

Don't fall for it, Tee, she told herself. *This is just your hormones talking. Don't be an idiot.* But somehow her inner voice didn't sound all that convincing.

"Tia? You might as well say yes because I'm not going to hang up until you do," Trent said.

"All right," Tia heard herself say. "How about we meet Wednesday around five-thirty?"

"I'll be there," Trent said. Damn, his voice was sexy.

As Tia hung up the phone, she caught sight of Angel's picture staring at her from the desk. "Don't look at me that way," she said. "I'm only going to meet him one more time—just for coffee. That way I can tell him everything in person."

Angel's photo gazed back at her silently.

"Okay, if you call me right now, I won't go," she said, glancing at the phone.

She counted to ten.

Then she counted to twenty.

Nothing. With an exasperated sigh Tia turned Angel's picture facedown against the desk and headed downstairs for a cookie.

Jessica pushed open the thick glass door into the school's main lobby on Monday morning. Her radar was on, searching the clusters of weary, postweekend students for a particular face. One with penetrating gray-blue eyes and dimples you could seriously fall into.

She had to find Will and talk to him before classes started. Things had been so tense and awkward over the weekend, and she wanted to get all that cleared up as soon as possible. No sense dragging all that stress into a new week.

Finally she spotted something familiar over by the trophy case. The signature baseball cap with curled brim, the trademark one-thumb-in-the-front-belt-loop slouch.

Jessica pushed her hair behind her ear. This was it. Time to be big. Time to forget about everything that happened and start over. She sauntered over as fast as her sling-back platforms would allow and threw her arms around him before he even saw her coming.

"I've been looking for you," she said, pulling back slightly so he would be sure to notice her warm, completely forgiving smile.

Will's expression was strangely unreadable. He almost looked . . . scared. But that wasn't possible. What did he have to be afraid of from her? Maybe he just needed more reassurance. No problem there.

Jessica closed her eyes and leaned in to plant a long kiss on his lips. But before their mouths could meet, Will's head jerked back and his shoulders stiffened.

"Don't," he whispered.

Jessica's eyes flew open. There was something about his tone that made her nerves sizzle. She peered at him, her face still only inches away from his. Suddenly he was as readable as a Dr. Seuss book. Will looked guilty. In fact, he could barely look her in the eye.

An icy sensation crept over Jessica. Something was up. Something bad.

"What is it?" she asked softly.

She could see his Adam's apple bounce up and down as he swallowed. Then he exhaled slowly and stared down at his feet. "We need to talk," he mumbled.

No, Jessica thought, her pulse accelerating. *I know what that means.*

"Look, is this about the party? Because I'm totally over that. Really. It was just one of those things, you know?" Her words came out high-pitched and fast, slurring together into one urgent-sounding tangle. She sounded pathetic, so she took a deep breath to try to calm herself.

"No," he said. "It's not about that."

Jessica stepped back and tilted her head slightly in a futile attempt to catch his downcast eyes. "Then what?" she asked. "What's going on?"

"It's just that . . ." Will's mouth closed tightly, and he was obviously clenching his teeth. He shifted his weight to his other leg and sighed. "Okay, look," he said finally. "There's really no easy way to say this, so here it is. . . . I can't see you anymore."

Jessica's heart seemed to cease beating, and a shudder ran through her from head to toe, threatening to take out her knees. Miraculously she managed to remain upright.

For the first time during the conversation Will looked at her. "I'm sorry," he said with not a shred of remorse in his voice. "But I . . ." He trailed off, glancing at something over Jessica's shoulder.

Turning around, Jessica caught a glimpse of Melissa standing by a row of lockers, pretending not to watch them. A searing blush spread across Jessica's face. Suddenly everything made sense.

"You're going back to her?"

Will briefly met her eyes and then glanced away.

"*Are* you?" she asked, more loudly. A nearby group of people turned to stare, but Jessica barely noticed.

Will nodded.

Jessica couldn't breathe. A tight pain spread across her chest, as if her heart were a wad of chewing gum stretched to the breaking point. How could this be happening? After everything they'd been through—everything she'd given up to have him. Was it all for nothing? Was he not even going to give this a decent chance?

Her knees trembled, and her entire body felt numb. More than anything, she wanted to run and hide—to make the entire, horrible scene disappear. But she made herself stop. She couldn't let him win.

Somehow she had to get in one good blow, then she could get away and cry in peace.

A fierce anger bubbled up from within. Jessica wasn't sure where the rage stemmed from—whether she was simply mad that he was dumping her for Melissa or that he didn't even have the decency to look her in the eye and say it in words. Either way, it gave her a pool of strength to dip into.

She stepped toward him, standing so completely in his airspace, he had no choice but to look at her. Then she hardened her gaze as best she could. "I understand," she replied flatly. "Obviously you're much weaker than I thought."

Unfortunately, instead of making her feel better, the whole thing left her drained and shaky. Mustering up what little stamina she had left, Jessica turned and walked away from Will, past Melissa's badly hidden smirk, and down the length of the corridor.

Then, finding a deserted spot behind a row of freshman lockers, she leaned against the wall and let the tears slip freely down her face.

"Hey, guys. Let me ask you a question. And I want you to be totally honest with me." Andy stared as earnestly as he could at his friends, who were gathered around the lunch table. Tia and Conner exchanged wary glances. But Maria, Ken, and Elizabeth all looked at him with obvious concern. At least some people took him seriously.

"Sure," Elizabeth said, setting down her fork. "What is it?"

Andy took in a breath and leaned back in his chair. "What do you think I'm good at?"

"Uh . . . what do you mean, exactly?" Tia asked.

Andy sighed, tipping back his chair so that he was balancing on the hind legs. "I mean, what do I excel at? What are my talents?" He wasn't sure how much plainer he could put it.

Conner snorted. "What's the catch?"

"Nothing," Andy replied irritably. "I'm serious. I want to know what you guys think."

"Well . . . ," Maria began, "you're funny."

"Okay. Okay. Great." Andy nodded. "What else?"

An awkward pause followed.

Andy glanced around at the confused faces of his friends and felt his cheeks start to flush. He slammed the front legs of his chair down. "Tia, you've known me forever. Tell me what else I'm good at."

"Um . . . well, you did teach me how to parallel park," she offered, raising her eyebrows.

"Uh-huh," Andy muttered. "So we've got jokes and parking. What else?"

Another pause. The sound of Maria sipping her milk was deafening.

"Okay, Andy," Conner broke in. "What's up?"

"Yeah. What's this all about?" Tia added.

Andy frowned down at his hamburger. "It's this college-prep stuff Mr. Nelson keeps going on about.

He says I have to join a club to show how well-rounded I am. Only I'm blank on ideas. And I doubt the school has a Joke Tellers Association or Future Car Parkers of America—not that they would look that great on a college application anyway."

Elizabeth waved a french fry at him. "Don't listen to us, Andy. You know yourself better than anyone. What do *you* think you're good at?"

Andy's eyes rolled upward as he pondered. "Let's see. . . . I'm a master at Nintendo, I play a mean Ping-Pong game, I can make my history teacher twitch uncontrollably. . . . Oh! And my mom says I'm the best one in the family at de–soap scumming the shower."

"Hmmm . . ." Elizabeth's brow furrowed for a moment, and then her eyes lit up. "I know!" she exclaimed. "How about the chess club?"

Tia and Conner burst out laughing, and Andy's blush deepened. He knew they were thinking the same thing he was, but it didn't change the fact that it sucked for them to think it.

"Liz, chess involves intelligence," Tia said jokingly, taking a sip of her Sprite.

It sucked even more for her to *say* it.

"Yeah," Andy agreed, trying to shrug it off. "I should've clarified—only games that involve joysticks."

"Hey! Maybe we could create some special job for you," Tia suggested, a glint of mischief in her eyes. "Like . . . you could be a library-official guy and go around shushing people."

"Or some cafeteria inspector, making sure all the workers have their hair nets properly on and stuff," Maria deadpanned.

Ken choked on a mouthful of food, laughing. "*That*'ll get him a scholarship."

"Face it, guys," Andy grumbled. "There's nothing out there for me. I should just prepare to make a living cleaning other people's showers."

Tia whacked him on the shoulder. "Oh, stop. There's lots of stuff you could do if you'd just try."

"Oh, yeah? Like what?" Andy asked. He started tearing his straw wrapper into tiny little pieces.

"Like . . . camping!" Tia said. "You love those trips you go on with your dad and Michael. We can never shut you up for about a month after you get back."

Andy shrugged, tearing the tiny wrapper pieces into tinier pieces. "So? I doubt they'll let me count those trips as extracurricular activities."

"What about the Outdoors Club?" Ken suggested.

"Exactly!" Tia put in, thrusting her hand out at Andy as if this answer was totally obvious.

"Outdoors Club?" Andy repeated. "What's that?"

Tia scowled. "They have posters up practically everywhere. Don't you read?"

"Sure." Andy shrugged. "Comic books, game manuals, the back of cereal boxes. But I don't pay much attention to the hallway propaganda."

"I cover their meetings sometimes for the paper,"

Elizabeth said, leaning back in her chair. "They meet Tuesdays after school in Mr. Watson's lab."

Andy rested his chin on his hand, feeling the color in his cheeks wash out for the first time in about ten minutes. The Outdoors Club. Maybe he should check it out.

"And if that doesn't work out, you could be the batboy for the softball team," Conner said. Everyone laughed, so Andy forced a chuckle. Maybe he should check out the Outdoors Club simply to shut up his friends.

Senior Poll Category #5:
Class Clown

Elizabeth Wakefield: Andy Marsden

Ken Matthews: Andy Marsden

Conner McDermott: Andy Marsden

Maria Slater: Andy Marsden

Jessica Wakefield: Andy Marsden

TIA RAMIREZ: ANDY MARSDEN

Will Simmons: Andy Marsden

melissa Fox: andy marsden

Andy Marsden: Conner McDermott

Never Let Them See You Sweat

Jessica checked the seams of her capri pants and smoothed the front of her blouse. Then she smoothed the back of her hair one last time and strode out of the girls' bathroom.

She really, *really* hated this. The first few post-breakup days (correction: post*dumping* days) could make or break you socially for weeks. It was only Tuesday, and rumors about Will dropping her for Melissa were no doubt already circulating. That meant people would be scrutinizing her more closely than ever. Showing her pain would only fuel the gossip. But if she acted overly cheerful, everyone would see through it. The best thing would be to act as subdued and nonchalant as she could.

She and Elizabeth had already rehearsed pat answers to the questions she'd be assaulted with all day long:

1. "I'd have to say I'm better off. Wouldn't you?"

2. "I never liked him *that* much. I mean, he picks his nose."

3. "Melissa's chains just kept getting in the way."

Okay, so it would definitely take some of her acting

ability to pull it off. But even if the carefree thing wasn't for real, at least it was how she *wanted* to feel. Maybe with enough practice it would sink in.

She glanced around and caught the first few stares of the day. Some morbidly curious. Some sympathetic. Nothing she couldn't handle.

So far, so good. Time to activate the Wakefield cool: chin high, chest up, detached expression of someone who has much more important things to think about than high school. If only she could find her friends. Or if she had another guy to walk the halls with. That would definitely make her feel better.

"Jessica! Over here!" Elizabeth's voice rose above the din in the hallway. Jessica caught a glimpse of her sister, standing by the bulletin board with Tia and Maria.

"Hey!" Jessica called, quickening her stride to join up with them.

"How's it going, Jess?" Maria asked.

Her stare triggered an upswell of self-pity, and Jessica quickly looked away, fiddling with her beaded bracelet. "I'm fine," she replied.

A brief yet awkward silence followed. "Your hair looks amazing," Tia said finally. "I love it when you wear it all twisted up like that."

Jessica grinned gratefully at Tia for changing the subject and boosting her ego all at once.

"Thanks," Jessica replied, her nerves slacking a little now that she had a distraction. "It's actually really easy. All you need is about a hundred bobby pins and half a can of hair spray."

Her friends laughed, and Jessica rolled back her shoulders, hoping to relax herself further. But her eyes still kept darting all over the place, searching for a glimpse of Will. Why did she want to torture herself?

"I'm thinking of growing mine out," Maria said, touching her hand to the back of her extremely short hair. "What do you guys think?"

"You know I like it short," Jessica said. "I've always thought—"

Suddenly Jessica completely lost her voice. She'd thought she'd mentally prepared herself, but from the force of her heart's reaction, her internal pep talks had fallen short.

Will and Melissa had walked in and were standing just a few yards away, leaning against the trophy case. They were both smiling. At each other. How could he? How could he go back to her?

Elizabeth, Maria, and Tia followed Jessica's gaze. Then they turned back toward Jessica, their faces tight with sympathy.

No! Jessica thought, starting to sweat. *Don't look at me that way. I've gotta stay cool!*

Without warning, Elizabeth laughed loudly and pushed Jessica lightly on the shoulder. "No way, Jess!" she said. "You mean he actually asked you out?"

It took Jessica a moment to snap to. "Oh . . . uh, yeah," she said after a beat. "He did. But I turned him down."

"I don't blame you," Maria jumped in. "I mean, you already have two dates lined up for this weekend. Any more than that would really confuse things."

"Well, you better get used to it." Tia tossed her long, dark hair over her shoulders. "You definitely made an impression at that Big Mesa party on Saturday."

Jessica laughed, a trickle of relief taking the edge off her panic. Looking as cool and nonchalant as possible, she leaned against the wall and glanced casually toward the trophy case. Will was staring right at her.

Melissa followed Will's gaze and said something into his ear. Then she grabbed his hand and pulled him down the hallway.

Jessica turned and watched them disappear down the corridor. It still hurt to see them. But at least she'd made it through this awkward moment. Maybe she could survive this after all.

She just had to take each triumph as it came— large or small.

"So, Tee, do you really think those guys from Big Mesa noticed me?"

Andy read the cardboard sign sitting on a chair outside the science lab:

OUTDOORS CLUB MEETING INSIDE

Hmmm. Sounds like an oxymoron, Andy thought. *With a name like that, you'd think they'd meet on the front lawn.*

He hesitated before opening the door. What would he find in there? Would the room be full of ripped people who looked like they'd walked straight out of a Honda Passport commercial? Would there be a chart inside the door that read, "You must be at least this high to join this club"?

Andy pushed through the door. About two dozen people were engaged in various conversations around the room. For a moment Andy thought that no one had noticed him.

"Hi!"

The voice was so loud, Andy had to hold his breath to keep from jumping. He glanced to his left, then down a few inches to find a girl smiling up at him. She looked only about five feet tall and no more than fifteen years old. Could the loud voice have come from her?

"This must be your first time," she said, eliciting a few snickers from a nearby group.

"Uh . . . yeah," he said. "Am I late?"

"Oh, no! We're just about to get started. Here!" She reached into a nearby satchel and pulled out a few colorful papers, which she handed over to him. "Here's a club roster, our club statement, and a list of activities we have planned this fall. Oh! And if you're interested, here's our official club insignia!"

The girl held up a decal depicting the sun peering out from behind a large cedar tree. The words *Sweet Valley High Outdoors Club* were printed underneath.

"Uh . . . thanks," Andy said, taking the sticker. *I wonder if these guys have a secret club handshake or birdcall greeting too.*

"Don't worry," the girl said, as if reading his mind. "We won't give you a test over the local wildlife or make you wear an official club pith helmet or anything."

Andy grinned. That sounded like something he might have said. Maybe he'd found his club after all.

"So what's your name?" she asked, cocking her head and twirling her long, strawberry-blond hair in a very little-girl-type gesture.

"Andy," he replied, feeling himself easing up a bit. "Andy Marsden."

"Hey, Travis!" the girl suddenly hollered, causing Andy's heart to freeze midbeat. "Come here and meet the new guy!"

A very blond, broad-shouldered, muscular guy strode up and offered his hand to Andy. Andy hesitated, fearing that a death squeeze from Conan the Barbarian might be some sort of club initiation ritual.

"Hi," Andy said, shaking Conan's hand. "Andy Marsden."

"Travis Hanson," the guy replied, gripping Andy's

hand in a firm yet bearable grasp. "President of the riffraff. We're about to start the meeting. Why don't you come up front and I'll introduce you? Then you can hang out and see if you like what you hear."

"Okay. Sure," Andy said.

They walked up to the front of the room, and the group immediately sat down and fell silent. Andy felt like a puny, pale scarecrow behind Travis's tanned, brawny frame. But he squared his shoulders, puffed up his chest, and tried to look like he belonged.

"I'd like to start off by introducing a new victim, Andy Marsden," Travis said with a laugh. "Everyone be nice to him, and maybe he'll decide to join."

Andy smiled halfheartedly as the crowd muttered "heys." Then, sensing the introductions were over, he quickly slunk into an empty chair in the front row.

Okay. That wasn't too bad, Andy thought. *I can probably make it through this meeting.*

"All right, then, moving on." Travis glanced down at a pad of paper in his hand. "As you probably know, the weather looks good for our hike up the Mesa Ridge this Sunday. This will be a great chance for us to try out the North Trail and do some more rock climbing."

Warning sirens went off in Andy's head. *Uh . . . did he say rock climbing?* As in hanging by a rope? Defying death? Breaking the law of gravity? Then again, maybe he didn't have to stay a whole meeting to figure out he was in the wrong place.

33

"Now, I think all of us are experienced in this type of climbing," Travis went on. "Except for maybe . . ." He carefully scanned the assembled members.

Andy tried to sink down in his seat.

"Andy, have you done any climbing?"

"Well . . . I'm the man to beat on the playground jungle gym," he replied, nervously raking his hand over the top of his head.

At least they laughed.

"Don't worry," Travis said, smiling. "Everyone here is at a different level of expertise, and no one is pressured into doing anything they're not yet trained for. So if you decide you want to become a member and come on this trip, we'll hook you up with a more experienced member for our first few outings."

Andy suddenly felt like everyone in the room was staring at him. "That sounds good," he said, before he even had the chance to think about it. "I'm in."

Travis smiled. "Spontaneous. I like it," he said. "Who would like to volunteer to be Andy's partner?"

Andy's resolve shrank to the size of a bread crumb. He could stomach the cutesy decal. He'd even managed to stand in front of the group without heaving up his lunch. But now he had to get paired up with a buddy? No way. What was this? Kindergarten?

Knowing his luck, he'd be matched with some extra-huge pea brain named Thor who would either (a) tease him relentlessly, (b) dare him to do some cliff diving on the first day, or (c) end up carrying him over his shoulder for most of the hike, thereby marring his manhood for years to come.

Forget it. Who cared about Mr. Nelson? College wasn't worth that much humiliation.

"I'll do it!" The same girl who had greeted him by the door stood up and smiled at him.

Andy smiled right back. *Her* he could handle.

"You've got a good one, Andy," Travis said, slapping the girl on the back. "Six took first place at Whiteface Peak's Climbing Death Match last year."

Six grinned. "Junior division," she said demurely.

Andy's head hit the desk. What was that Conner said about becoming a batboy?

Angel sat down at his dorm-room desk and opened his computer-science textbook. At least he *thought* he was at his desk. He hadn't really seen the top of it in several days.

He leaned back in his chair, propped up his feet, and tried to concentrate on the latest chapter.

Interface—*A connecting link that allows independent systems to communicate with each other.*

Communicate . . . he'd been having some trouble with that lately. He really, really, *really* needed to call Tia.

Just in the past week he'd received one package, two letters, six phone messages, and eight e-mails.

He'd only gotten one letter from his own mother—and two paragraphs of that were devoted to how much Tia seemed to miss him.

A beep from his computer suddenly snapped him out of his thoughts. Glancing up at the screen, he noticed the You've Got Mail sign flashing in the corner. He clicked onto his in-box menu and recognized Tia's address.

Make that *nine* e-mails yet to be answered.

Angel sighed and activated the screen saver. He couldn't write to her right now—not when he had to read and outline this chapter and then study for Wednesday's quiz. She'd written him so many long, in-depth e-mails, he knew he'd feel bad if he didn't put time and effort into responding. And there was no way Tia was going to stand for a "Hey, baby! I miss you. I love you. Love, Angel," in response to a five-page ramble on how much she missed the scent of his cologne.

Maybe he'd have time later if he wasn't too tired. He was already having a tough time keeping his eyes open to read.

He let out a long, deep yawn and stretched his arms. Then he sat back in his chair and stared at his textbook, propping his feet on the desk.

A knock sounded on the door. "Yo, Angel." Cody Benton, his next-door neighbor, poked his head into the room. "We're all taking a break and heading out for pizza. You in?"

The thought of a warm slice of pepperoni

supreme recharged Angel's energy stores. Maybe if he got some food in him, he'd be able to stay up long enough to finish his work. "Yeah. I'm there," he replied, tilting upright in his chair. "Just let me shut down my computer. I'll meet you at the elevators."

"Okay." Cody closed the door, and Angel could hear the guys' muffled talk grow fainter as they headed down the hall.

He snapped his computer book shut, threw it on the desk, and went to shut down his computer. A slight pang of guilt passed through him when he saw Tia's e-mail header staring back at him. Angel quickly clicked the Write Mail icon. His fingers flew across the keyboard.

```
From: a.desmond@stanford.edu
To: tee@swiftnet.com
Time: 10:45 p.m.
Subject: Miss you

    Hey, baby!
    I miss you. I love you.
                    Love,
                    Angel
```

He clicked the send button, knowing she wasn't going to be satisfied with his response but feeling better that he'd at least done something.

Okay. So maybe he should have taken more time. But a guy's gotta eat, right?

*   *   *

As the Outdoors Club meeting disbanded, Andy's new climbing partner met him at the doorway.

"Hey! So what did you think?" she asked, bouncing up to him. "How was your first official meeting?"

Andy took in her clear green eyes, thick, strawberry-blond hair, and perfect, pink-hued complexion. She reminded him of one of those Cabbage Patch Kids, only grown-up.

"Not bad," he replied. "I'm glad no one made me wear a name tag—that earns you guys big points."

She laughed, tossing her ponytail behind her shoulders. Andy smiled. It was good to have a new, appreciative audience. The best reaction his jokes got from his friends lately were snarls and eye rolling.

"Hey, glad you came." Travis came up behind him and clapped him on the back.

"Yeah," Andy replied.

"Should be a cool hike Sunday. I hope all our talk about safety precautions didn't make you chicken out or anything."

"No way, man," Andy said, trying to sound determined.

The last wave of club members were heading through the door. Andy, Travis, and Six stepped in behind them, filing out into the hallway.

"Well, catch you later," Travis said as he headed down the corridor. Then he turned and nodded toward Andy's partner. "See you at home."

"Yeah. Later," she called.

"You're his sister?" Andy asked, staring from the girl to Travis's disappearing frame.

"Yeah. I'm Six," she said, holding out her hand. "Six Hanson."

He grasped her palm and shook it, astonished by the strength in her tiny grip. "Hey, cool name. Sounds sort of like a *Star Wars* android or something. Is it your real name or just something people call you?"

"Oh, it's real," she replied, nodding. "I'm the last of six kids, and I guess my folks were just too tired to think up a name by the time I came along."

Andy let out a low whistle. "Whoa. You have five brothers and sisters?"

"Yep," she replied. "Travis's closest to my age. The rest are off at college." She shouldered a bulging blue backpack and headed out into the hall. Andy fell into step beside her.

"So, is your whole family into hiking and stuff?" Andy asked.

"Oh, yeah!" she exclaimed. "We practically grew up in tents and sleeping bags. My parents' idea of a family vacation was white-water rafting down the Colorado River or salmon fishing in the Matanuska Valley. How about you?"

"We went camping and everything, but the most adventure we saw was on the roller coasters at Disneyland," Andy said. "So even with six kids I take it your folks aren't much like Mr. and Mrs. Brady, huh?"

"No way!" Six exclaimed with a laugh. "My dad's an anthropology professor at Orange County Community College, and my mom runs Hanson's Sporting Goods. I work with her part-time. Oh, *hey!*" Her volume suddenly increased, and she reached over and grabbed Andy's wrist. "That reminds me! Do you need any supplies for our hike on Sunday?"

Andy hadn't even thought of the equipment issue. It had been a while since his family went camping, and most of their stuff was either broken, lost, or embarrassingly outdated.

"Uh, well . . . except for a pair of rad sunglasses, I'm afraid I'm pretty poor on hiking equipment."

"Then you should come by our shop!" Six said, tightening her grip. "I'll fix you up with everything you need. And I'll give you a discount too!"

"Really? That'd be cool," Andy replied.

She grinned gigantically, revealing a set of perfect, commercial-worthy teeth. "No problem! I'm working on Saturday afternoon. You should stop by."

"Okay," he said with a shrug. "Sounds great."

"Great!" she echoed.

They stopped walking and stood smiling at each other for a moment. Andy could sense that the conversation had completely tapered off. But before he could excuse himself, Six slapped herself on the forehead.

"I'm such an idiot!" she exclaimed. "I'm, like,

telling you everything about me, and you haven't had a chance to say anything." She thumped her forefinger against her left temple. "What a ditz, huh? When you have a million brothers and sisters, you tend to hog the conversation as much as you can. And yes, that's also why I'm so loud, if you were wondering."

Andy laughed. "Are you loud? I hadn't noticed."

"Yeah, right. So . . . ," she said, moving her hands in rolling motion. "Come on. Out with it. What other clubs and stuff are you into?"

"Let's see. . . ." Andy rubbed his chin dramatically. "I'm also a member of the Indoors Club, the Club Sandwich Club, and the Club Club. That last group meets at the Riot every Friday night."

"Very funny," she said, giggling.

"Okay, not really. But my friends and I usually hang out there on Fridays."

"Cool," Six said, tightening the straps on her backpack. "I've never been there."

"Really?" Andy asked. "Then why don't you come hang out with us this Friday? We don't have an official decal or anything, but our meetings are fun."

"No name tags?" she asked, her eyes twinkling.

"No name tags."

"Then I'd love to!" Six said.

Andy couldn't help but chuckle. "Great," he said, holding up the papers in his hand. "I'll check your number on the roster and call you later with the details. Okay?"

"Cool!" She turned and headed down the hallway. "Talk to you later!"

Andy gave her a wave and headed in the opposite direction. Wow. His friends were definitely going to get a kick out of that girl. So what if she was loud, perky, and somewhat cutesy? At least she had a sense of humor.

Lila Fowler

I'm not exactly a history buff or anything (I know that comes as a total shock), but I did take an occasional note last year in Mr. Jansen's class. One lecture I remember as being less than brain-deadeningly boring was the one on how European countries took sides during the world wars. That I could relate to. I mean, finally— something you can use in real life. You've got to have allies if you want any power at all in high school.

Anyway, I keep thinking about that lecture lately and how Italy started out on one side, then—when it looked like they were going to get their butts kicked—suddenly changed teams. To me it always seemed like smart thinking. That's what I did at the start of the school year when it became apparent that the Great and Wonderful Jessica Wakefield was headed for a major fall—I joined up with the opposition. Smart, huh?

Only suddenly it doesn't seem so smart. People are wa-a-ay tired of the Will-Melissa drama. And somehow Jessica has come out of the whole mess totally untouched. In fact, people seem more intrigued by her than ever.

The winds of war are turning again. If this keeps up, I may have to pull another Italy.

Girls Just Wanna Have Fun

4

Jessica walked through the side door of the house and tiptoed inside, hoping to steer clear of any human contact. No such luck. When she rounded the corner into the kitchen, she found her mom sitting at the table, talking on the phone.

"Hi, honey! How was school?" Mrs. Wakefield asked, moving the receiver away from her mouth.

"Fine," Jessica muttered, trying to avoid eye contact. She quickly set down her book bag and pretended to retie her shoelace. Luckily her mom was too busy with her phone call to press for more information. She had no idea her daughter was seconds away from total disintegration.

Jessica had nothing against her mother at the moment—or any member of the family. She was simply on the verge of a major self-pity fest. And she was too exhausted to explain what was wrong and too exhausted to pretend everything was fine.

Somehow she had managed to get through one more day of school, pretending she was over Will dumping her. In fact, her shields managed to hold up pretty well. She got through history class without even making eye contact with him, ate lunch with her friends in a secluded spot in the courtyard, and even supported Melissa without the slightest tremble as they practiced their pyramid during cheerleading. But after school, just as she was congratulating herself on her superb acting ability, she'd headed out to the parking lot and seen Will and Melissa leaning against his Blazer, kissing. Jessica had managed to find the strength to act natural instead of blowing chunks all over the hot asphalt, but the effort had sapped all her energy.

Jessica grabbed a handful of Oreo cookies out of the pantry and headed upstairs to her room.

Pillow. That was all she wanted. A few cookies and a big, fluffy pillow to hug. Nothing more. Who cared if it was only five-thirty? As far as she was concerned, the day was over. Might as well turn in now.

She didn't even get to the first Oreo before the tears came. The second she reached the seclusion of her room, she flopped down on her bed and cried.

Two days. It's only been two days, she thought miserably. *How am I going to make it through the week?*

"Jess?"

She lifted her head and saw Elizabeth hovering over her, a look of concern creasing her features.

"Are you okay?" Elizabeth asked.

Jessica groaned. "Leave me alone."

Elizabeth walked toward the bed. Jessica couldn't

help but notice how flawless her sister looked, even after a full day of school. Even though she was giving Jessica the concerned head tilt, Elizabeth still had that special I've-got-a-boyfriend glow.

Jessica groaned and buried her face in her pillow. That was the last thing she needed to see right now.

"I heard you crying from my room," Elizabeth explained, pushing her blond hair behind her ears and crossing her arms over her chest. "Do you want to talk about it?"

"No," Jessica said into the pillow.

Elizabeth sat down on the bed. She never had been very good at taking a hint.

"You know, I feel really guilty about this whole thing," Elizabeth mumbled. "I wish I'd never pushed you to go out with him."

"It's not your fault," Jessica said softly. "*I* got myself in this mess. He fooled all of us into thinking he was actually a cool person." Her voice broke, and a new round of tears streamed down her face. "Even Mom liked him."

"Yeah, well, not after she heard what he did to you. I think she threw out the plant he gave her," Elizabeth said.

Jessica snorted a tear-filled laugh. "Really?"

"Yep." Elizabeth put her hand on Jessica's arm. "Listen, you just have to try to remember all the negatives. I mean, I know it's hard, but—"

"Look, I'm *trying*, okay?" Jessica snapped. "I'd just . . . I'd *really* like to be alone."

But Elizabeth didn't budge. For a moment she sat there quietly. Then, just when Jessica was about to lose her temper entirely, Elizabeth leaned toward the bed and added, "You know, you could always look on the bright side."

Jessica raised her head and narrowed her eyes at her sister. "Bright side?"

"At least we're not still living at the Fowlers'," Elizabeth said. "I mean, can you imagine? You'd have Lila listening to you through the wall, taking notes. And Mrs. Pervis would be barging in to do all the important dusting or something. Here you actually have some privacy."

"Oh, really?" Jessica mumbled. "Not as far as I can see."

Hint number two missed its mark as well. Elizabeth stood up and grabbed the phone from Jessica's desk.

"What are you doing?" Jessica asked, sitting up and pushing her tangled hair out of her eyes.

"Calling in the troops," Elizabeth replied. "You've done enough wallowing for one day."

Jessica closed her eyes and sighed. Maybe she should suggest her sister look up the word *alone*.

The moment Tia walked through the door of House of Java and spotted Trent at the front counter, talking with Jeremy, she felt a flutter of first-date jitters. Weird. She hadn't experienced that sensation in years.

Get a grip, she told herself as she straightened her cheerleading sweatshirt. It wasn't like they were on a date. In fact, she was there to tell him they never would be.

Trent laughed, and the flutter intensified. He was better looking than she'd remembered. Deep brown skin, broad shoulders, dark eyes rimmed with thick, black lashes. Even his shaved head didn't bother her. Funny. She had always assumed hair was a prerequisite for a guy's good looks. But Trent's cue-ball style only seemed to draw more attention to his eyes and smile.

"You're going to get yourself in trouble," Tia muttered, shaking her head. She moved toward the counter, endeavoring for a casual walk. "Hey, guys," she said when she reached Trent's side.

"Hey, Tia," Jeremy said.

Trent's whole face brightened. "Tia! Thought for a second you weren't gonna show," Trent said, looking so laid-back and confident, she didn't believe his words for a moment. "You want something to drink?"

"Yeah, I'll take a cappuccino." Tia opened up her purse for her wallet, but Trent laid a hand on her arm.

"Uh-uh. This is on me." He fished a five-dollar bill out of the pocket of his varsity jacket and slid it across the counter. "Aames, could you get the lady a cappuccino?" he asked, watching her the entire time.

Tia felt her mouth twitching at the sides. There was something about the way he looked at her that made her temperature spike. And the thing was, she sort of liked it. She couldn't remember the last time anyone, including Angel, had stared at her like that. Sending Trent away might end up being harder than she thought.

"Here you go," Jeremy said, pushing a freshly steamed cappuccino across the counter. He grinned at Tia and winked. "You guys have fun."

Tia felt a slight blush rise to her cheeks. Did Jeremy assume she and Trent were *together*? If he did, he might say something to Jessica, and then Jessica would come back to her and ask about Angel, and then—

It was time for her to set the record straight.

Tia led the way to a secluded corner booth and slid onto the smooth, velvet seat. "Trent? I'm just gonna lay it on the line here," she said. "That whole kissing thing at the party was a big mistake."

Trent stared down at his drink. "I know."

"You what?" Tia asked. Her heart actually gave a painful thump. She wasn't expecting this to be *easy*.

"Look, I'm sorry," Trent said, laying his forearms on the surface of the table—his very well-toned forearms. "I don't normally move that fast. I mean, not when I really like someone. From here on out, I promise to take things more slowly."

Tia froze, letting his words sink in. *Really like someone? From here on out?* Could he be any more flattering?

"So when can I see you again?" Trent asked, his eyes sparkling.

Tia arched one eyebrow. "That's your version of taking it slow?"

"I hold the county record in the hundred-yard dash," Trent said with another pulse-altering grin. "I have a skewed definition of slow."

Tia was concentrating so hard on controlling her blush and keeping herself from smiling, she couldn't find a snappy comeback. She was totally thrown. This *never* happened to her.

"What about Saturday?" Trent said, sipping his coffee.

"Trent, I . . ."

She couldn't believe the way he was looking at her. He was looking at her like he'd never seen anything so rivetingly beautiful in his life. Tia glanced helplessly at the ceiling, trying to avoid his gaze.

"Come on. Nothing fancy," he said, lowering his voice into an almost whisper. "We'll just hang out somewhere and talk."

She forced herself to meet his gaze, heard a tiny voice inside her head saying, "Yes, you idiot, say yes!" and jumped up from her seat.

"I have to go," she said, hurrying past him. "Thanks for the coffee."

"Tia!" he called after her. She heard him sliding out of the booth. "Can I call you?" He didn't even sound thrown by the fact that she was running off two minutes after she arrived. Why did she find that overconfidence so damned attractive?

Tia paused at the door, one hand on the knob, *this close* to freedom. This close to a guilt-free existence.

She turned around, flashed a quick, tight smile, and said, "You have my number. It's up to you how you use it."

Before she fled, she got one last glimpse of Trent's widening smile. Of Jeremy holding his hand over the counter for a high five.

It figured the one good line she did come up with was the one that took her in the completely wrong direction.

Jessica closed her eyes against the bright light of the television. *Will and Melissa. Will's back with Melissa.* No matter what her sister did to try to distract her, Jessica's brain wouldn't stop repeating the names. *Will and Melissa. Melissa and Will.* Even *Flashdance,* one of the cheesiest movies ever made, wasn't doing the trick.

"Don't let those clothes ever come back in style," Elizabeth said from her sprawled position on the sofa.

"Please," Jessica replied, keeping her eyes closed.

"You have nothing to worry about, Liz. You never wear anything the fashion magazines tell you to anyway."

Elizabeth chucked a pillow at Jessica's head. "I was concerned about you . . . and the fact that if you ever wore leg warmers and rubber bracelets, I'd have to disown you as a sister."

Jessica allowed herself a smirk. "Right. Like you could ever live without me," she said, propping the pillow behind her head.

"I hate to interrupt this Hallmark moment, but this is the best part," Maria said, adjusting her position in the big, comfy armchair so that her long legs were hanging over the side. The three girls watched with convulsive giggles as Jennifer Beals took off her bra under her shirt, leaving the guy she was with drooling.

"Oh, yeah. That's sexy," Jessica said sarcastically, rolling her eyes.

"Liz? Can't we move on?" Maria asked, covering her eyes with her hand. "I know you've got every Tom Cruise movie ever made. That stupid pool movie would be better than this."

"Hey! Don't knock *The Color of Money*," Elizabeth said, glaring comically at Maria. "It's bad, but not bad enough for tonight's lineup."

Jessica shook her head. Of all the bizarre themes her sister had thought up for a girls' night, this one, "Mallomars and Bad Movies of the Eighties," had to take the top prize.

"We have to watch the movies we rented," Elizabeth said, sitting up and hitting the pause button. She sorted through the tapes on the coffee table as Jessica shoved an entire Mallomar in her mouth. "I've got *Eddie and the Cruisers, Teen Wolf,* and *Xanadu,* with Olivia Newton-John."

Jessica groaned through a mouthful of goo and chocolate. "I thought you guys wanted to cheer me up. Where are the hot guys?"

Maria ran her fingers through her short, black hair, causing it to stick straight up. "I thought the whole purpose of this night was to get your mind *off* hot guys."

"Nice one, Maria," Elizabeth said, nudging her with her foot. Jessica felt her sister glance at her but avoided eye contact. "Will's not *that* hot," Elizabeth said.

Jessica cracked a smile.

"Yeah, and what's up with the baseball hat?" Maria said, planting her feet on the floor and leaning forward. "I mean, hello? Doesn't he know that constant hat wearing promotes baldness?"

"Seriously?" Jessica said with a laugh.

"Yeah!" Elizabeth exclaimed. "You know he's going to end up with a beer gut, a double chin, a bald spot, and a bad polyester suit, chomping on some gross cigar and telling everyone at his life-insurance firm that he was a huge star in high school."

Jessica doubled over at the image. Sometimes her

articulate sister and her sarcastic friend really came in handy.

"And you know Melissa will be cracking the whip the entire time," Maria said. She mimicked picking up the phone. "Will, bring home some diapers for our four bratty, spoiled kids, Mel, Melinda, Melanie, and Melissa Junior, and don't forget to pick up my clothes at the dry cleaner, and—"

"Honey?" Elizabeth interrupted in a low, yet desperate voice, holding her own imaginary phone. "Uh, Melissa? Melissa, sweetie? Could I please relieve my bladder now? Melissa? Would it be all right if I exhale?"

Jessica couldn't take it anymore. She burst out laughing, tears streaming down her face. Elizabeth and Maria lost it too, and for a moment there was nothing but the sound of hysterical laughter and Maria slapping her hand against the table.

And for a moment there were zero thoughts of Will.

Maria Slater's List of
Postbreakup Pick-me-ups

1. A huge serving of Ben & Jerry's Phish Food
2. A good cry
3. A whole pint of Ben & Jerry's Chunky Monkey
4. Any movie where a lying, cheating guy gets it bad in the end
5. A whole gallon of Ben & Jerry's Coffee Toffee Crunch
6. Taking any mementos or gifts he gave you and ripping, breaking, flushing, torching, or shooting them with a weapon
7. A truck full of Ben & Jerry's Cherry Garcia
8. Tae-bo workouts—especially when you visualize your ex-boyfriend's face as you do your kicks
9. Working to pass some sort of legislation that banishes all men from this country
   Except Ben and Jerry. They can stay.

Mustard, mayonnaise, leftover eggplant Parmesan, pickles, grapes, Swiss cheese . . . where the heck was all the sweet stuff? Did they eat it all last night?

Jessica stood in the open doorway of her family's refrigerator, carefully scanning the inventory. She'd made it through another day of school without breaking down, and she wanted to reward herself with a treat—preferably something it would take her a ten-mile jog to work off.

She tried the freezer for the second time, hoping a pint of Häagen-Dazs would miraculously appear behind the frozen broccoli. No luck.

What was wrong with this family? Was she the first one to have a personal crisis since moving day? Pudding, chocolate sauce, and a spare DoveBar should always be kept around the house in case of emergencies.

"Hey, Jess!" Elizabeth came running into the room, her face flushed and her button-down shirt completely disheveled. She looked like she'd just run in from a hot date or something. "Guess what just happened!"

"Why should I?" Jessica quipped irritably. This was too much spunk to take without any sugar in her own system.

"Conner just called!" Elizabeth exclaimed.

"So?" Jessica wrinkled her nose. "Big deal. That happens pretty much hourly, doesn't it?"

Elizabeth rolled her eyes. "Just listen, okay? Conner got a phone call from that guy Jack Leary who books all the bands for House of Java. Apparently someone canceled at the last minute for tonight's gig and Jack wants Conner to fill in!"

"Wow," Jessica remarked, trying to sound enthused. "That's great, Liz."

"He's like a real working musician!" Elizabeth said, doe-eyed. *You'd think she'd just gotten a call from Dave Matthews himself,* Jessica thought.

But she couldn't help smiling. In a way, it grated on her nerves to see Elizabeth hopping with excitement, her face all lit up like a halogen lamp. And it struck her as mildly off-kilter. Usually Elizabeth was the cool, calm one and Jessica was constantly bubbling over. Still, just because Jessica had no reason to be so psyched up didn't mean she couldn't be happy for Elizabeth. At least someone in the family had a life at the moment.

"So you're coming tonight," Elizabeth said. It was a statement, not a question.

"Me? At Conner's gig?" Jessica asked.

Elizabeth frowned. "Sure. Why not?"

"I don't know, Liz. I just don't really feel like it." She turned around and opened the pantry door, searching desperately for any package marked Chocolate Covered or Cream Filled.

"Come on. It'll be fun," Elizabeth urged, stepping into the doorway and blocking Jessica's view. "Besides, you told us last night you were ready to move on with your life. This is your chance."

"But I'm exhausted!" Jessica exclaimed, leaning against the door frame. "I spent all day doing the healthy, high-road thing again and fried. All I want to do is lie down and veg."

Elizabeth raised her eyebrows, and the impatient, somewhat patronizing look Jessica was all too familiar with crept onto her sister's face. "Didn't you have fun last night?" Elizabeth asked. "Didn't you agree it was better to be social and forget your problems for a while?"

"Yeah, but . . ." Jessica's eyes darted around the room, as if she could find an excuse stamped out on the new kitchen wallpaper. "But what if I run into Jeremy there?" she said quickly. "That could be awkward."

Elizabeth shook her head. "You and I both know Jeremy would be nothing but nice to you. Plus if he is there, he'll be too busy working to spend time with us."

She had her there. Jessica was fast running out of excuses, and Elizabeth knew it.

"Besides," Elizabeth added, "Tia and Andy have already spread the word through the El Carro and Big Mesa crowd. The place will be crawling with cute guys."

Jessica sighed. She knew Elizabeth was just trying to boost her morale, but the last thing Jessica wanted right now was to get tangled with some new guy.

Elizabeth reached past her and grabbed a bag of pretzels off the pantry shelf. "This is the perfect opportunity for you to meet people and show the world that Will Simmons means nothing to you," she went on, her words growing muffled as she crunched down on a couple of pretzels. "You have to go."

"No, Liz. Not this time," Jessica said wearily, plopping down into a nearby chair.

A pretzel suddenly bounced off her head.

"You're going if Conner, Tia, and Maria have to help me physically drag you in there," Elizabeth announced, "so you might as well go upstairs and change."

Jessica's mouth fell open.

"I know you think I'm bluffing, but I assure you, I'm not." Elizabeth plunked another pretzel into her mouth, spun on her heels, and sauntered out of the room.

Jessica put her head down on the table. She *really* didn't want to go to House of Java. But what could she do? It wasn't like she had the strength to fight Elizabeth on the matter. Besides, the last thing she needed in her life right now was more conflict.

So she'd go. She'd hate it, but she'd go.

Maybe it wouldn't be so bad. After all, at least they had cake there.

Tia turned off the cordless phone and set it on its base. Then she immediately picked it back up again. Angel had finally responded to her e-mails—sort of. He hadn't actually *responded* to anything she'd told him, but at least he'd taken a second to write to her. Now she wanted to talk to him more than ever.

But she'd already left three messages on his machine. Should she try him again? Maybe he'd tried to call her back while she was tying up the line for the last half hour, telling everyone to come see Conner. Maybe she should just check and see if he was home. If the machine answered, she'd know he hadn't called.

She turned on the phone and punched out the numbers she knew by heart. One ring . . . two rings . . . three rings . . . Eventually she heard a click followed by Angel's tape-recorded voice. "Hi. This is Angel. I'm not in right now, but if you'll leave a—"

Tia quickly turned off the phone. No need to leave yet another message and look totally whipped. She held the receiver against her chest and flopped back on the bed. Just hearing his voice—even on tape—made her pulse speed like a runaway train. God, she missed him! She had known all along it would be hard with him gone, but not *this* hard. She never expected it would make her physically ache.

The digital numbers on her desk clock switched to seven thirty-two. What exactly was he doing anyway? Classes were over, the campus store where he worked closed at six, and Angel never ate dinner this late.

Maybe he was at one of those wild frat parties they always showed in the movies, where everyone ended up naked in the swimming pool. Or maybe some cute coed invited him to her place to study . . .

"Stop it," she muttered pressing her hands against her eyes.

A harsh rapping sound interrupted her thoughts.

"Yeah?" she replied flatly.

The door opened, and her mother came into the room. "Honey, we need to talk," she said solemnly.

Tia pushed herself upright and stared at her mother's frowning face. She wore that stiff, I'm-trying-hard-not-to-yell-my-lungs-out type of expression, and her hands gripped a bulging envelope as if it were a weapon.

"What's wrong, Mom?" Tia asked tentatively.

"I want you to see what came in the mail today." She pulled a stack of papers out of the envelope and handed them to Tia. It was their latest phone bill. "Notice the amount due at the bottom of this page," she said, pointing.

Tia followed her mother's fingertip. The number in the red "total" box said $223.78. Tia's mouth dropped open. "That much?" she asked.

"Oh, yes," her mother replied. Then she lifted away the top page. "Now, this next section will show you why the bill is so high. I want you to look it over carefully."

Tia scanned down the long list of itemized calls. A few were to her grandparents in San Antonio, but all the rest were to Stanford. It seemed like she'd phoned Angel almost every single day since he left, ten times a day. There were an insane number of one-minute calls when she got his answering machine, peppered with a few much longer (and expensive) ones when she actually got ahold of him.

A cold, numbing sensation washed over her. So here it was. Undeniable proof that she had actually lost her mind.

"God, Mom. I'm sorry," she whispered guiltily. "I had no idea."

Mrs. Ramirez sat on the bed and put a consoling arm around her daughter. "I know, honey. And I know how much you miss Angel. I do too. So do the boys. But you have to cut back on all this calling. We just can't afford it."

"I know," Tia mumbled. "I promise I'll be better. I'll just have to e-mail him more often instead."

Concern plaited her mother's forehead. "Honey, I know you want to keep in close touch with him. But you have to understand that he's very busy right now and he doesn't have much time to talk."

"I already know that!" Tia snapped. Or at least

her brain knew it. Her heart was having a tough time accepting it as fact.

"Hey," her mother said, giving Tia a reassuring pat on the leg. "That doesn't mean he loves you any less. It's his job to concentrate on college right now. And it's your job to understand it."

Tia sighed irritably. Why couldn't her mother be completely clueless like parents were supposed to be? How was it she knew exactly the way Tia felt? Was she just psychic in a freaky, motherly sort of way? Or was Tia just that obvious?

"Well, I'll let you get ready," her mother said, standing. "I'm so glad you're going out and having fun tonight instead of sitting around missing Angel and calling him every hour."

"Yeah," Tia said, laughing nervously. No need to tell her about the four calls she'd made earlier.

As Mrs. Ramirez headed out the door, Tia called, "Hey, Mom? You know, I have some money saved up. I'll help you pay for the bill."

Her mother smiled. "I know, hon. We'll work that out later. You go have fun." Then she walked out, shutting the door behind her.

Tia snatched the phone bill off her bedspread and stared at it again. A sick feeling welled up in the pit of her stomach. This wasn't her making all those calls. This was someone else—a desperate, clingy girl who felt worthless without her boyfriend.

She'd always known girls like that. The ones who

kept tabs on their guys at all times, planned their lives around them, and threw fits worthy of an Academy Award if they didn't return a call or stared two seconds too long at some other girl.

Tia had always pitied them and prided herself on her enlightened attitude. Now here she was, playing the same stupid games.

She had to stop this fast. Before she completely lost Angel's respect. And her own.

"Come on, Jess. Jess? Jess!"

Jessica glanced up at her sister, who was gesturing wildly from the middle of the parking lot. Why couldn't she just chill? Conner wasn't supposed to start playing for another fifteen minutes. Besides, it wasn't like this was a once-in-a-lifetime concert event.

"Excuse me a sec while I lock up the Jeep," Jessica called, shouldering her handbag and commencing a lackadaisical trudge toward the café.

"What's wrong?" Elizabeth asked, putting a hand on Jessica's arm. "I thought you said you were determined to have fun tonight."

"I said I would *try* to have fun," Jessica replied.

Elizabeth smiled. "Okay. I'm just glad you decided to come." She hooked an arm through Jessica's and propelled her toward the front entrance.

They pushed through the door and glanced around at the assembled crowd. Already a sizable fraction of all three high-school populations were milling around the café, waiting for the show to start.

"Oh my God!" Elizabeth exclaimed. "Can you believe how many people are here? Conner's going to be so psyched!"

"Yeah," Jessica replied sarcastically. "Because 'psyched' is an emotion Conner often conveys."

Elizabeth rolled her eyes as Jessica warily scanned the crowd. She was almost positive Will and Melissa wouldn't be here. Conner's gigs didn't attract their crowd. Still, she should make certain, just so she didn't get caught off guard.

After a careful search, she assured herself that the Wonder Couple were nowhere near the place. But a familiar figure behind the counter made her freeze. Jeremy was here. In fact, he was looking right at her.

A small flutter welled up in Jessica's stomach. Surely by now he'd heard about Will breaking up with her. What would he do? She just couldn't handle a look of pity or an I-told-you-so type of glance.

Jessica ducked her head and stared at the wall, pretending to be studying a flyer about egg donors, until Elizabeth started yanking her in the opposite direction.

"Hey, Jess!" Jeremy said with a totally normal smile as she and Elizabeth passed the long line at the counter.

"Hey," Jessica said back.

Elizabeth steered Jessica toward the courtyard doorway. "See? I told you he'd be nice." Jessica shrugged. "Now, come on," Elizabeth continued. "I want a table down front."

They entered the tree-lined courtyard, where Conner was already setting up his microphone on the wooden platform in the corner. The tables were packed, and little white lights twinkled from the fence surrounding the yard. Jessica took a deep breath. Maybe this wouldn't be so bad.

"I'm going to go wish Conner luck," Elizabeth said. "You grab us a table, okay?" Then, before Jessica could respond, Elizabeth trotted off toward the stage, her little black skirt bouncing as she went.

Jessica's heart dropped, and she suddenly felt horribly conspicuous. As sad as it was arriving on the arm of her sister, it was definitely preferable to standing there alone in the middle of a sociably loud crowd. She got the sinking sensation that everyone was looking at her instead of the stage. *Look at Jessica, guyless and left out. Remember when she used to have a life?*

"Hey, Jess!" a familiar voice called out. She glanced up and saw Andy Marsden's freckled face grinning at her from a large table right down in front. "Over here!"

She couldn't remember ever being this glad to see Andy. Not only was he saving her from imminent ridicule, but he'd also fulfilled Elizabeth's table request. *From now on,* she promised herself, *he'll be on my list of top-ten favorite people.* There had been an opening since Will had flaked out anyway.

Jessica settled down in an empty chair next to Andy. On his other side sat an unfamiliar guy—at least she assumed it was a guy—with long, shaggy hair partially hiding his face. He was leaning back dangerously far in the wooden café chair, his feet propped up on the stage. Jessica glanced at him as covertly as possible, taking in every detail of his bizarre attire. He wore a tattered black T-shirt, plaid shorts baggy enough to hang glide in, and shoes so full of holes, the laces had to be the only things holding them together.

What's Andy doing with one of the grunge burnouts? she wondered. *Shouldn't this guy be skateboarding underneath the Majela overpass?*

Oh, well. At least she had a crowd to hang with. Beggars can't be choosers.

"Jess, this is Evan Plummer," Andy said, gesturing at the creature next to him. "He's from El Carro. Evan, this is Jessica Wakefield, a Sweet Valley original."

"Hey." The mound of hair nodded at her. "You're Elizabeth's sister?"

"Right," she replied, smiling at the latitude where she imagined his eyes might be.

"Cool. Elizabeth is a cool girl."

"Thanks," Jessica said. "I mean . . . I think so too."

Evan suddenly pushed away from the table, his right hand digging into a cavernous pocket for his billfold. "Hey, save my seat, all right?" he said to Andy. "I'm gonna grab a drink before the show starts." Then he loped off toward the café.

"Ooookay," Jessica said once Evan had disappeared from sight. "What rock did he crawl out from under?"

"Evan?" Andy asked, seemingly surprised. "Oh, he's cool. He just forgets to shower sometimes."

Jessica laughed. "How exactly do you know him?"

"You've never seen him around school?" Andy asked. Jessica shook her head. *That* guy went to SVH?

"He lives across the street from me," Andy explained, taking a sip from his steaming coffee mug. "He comes over a lot to use our pool for workouts. The guy's fanatical about swimming."

At least that means he occasionally immerses in clean water, Jessica thought.

"Actually, I think Evan had a crush on Liz before. Didn't she tell you? We all went to this concert together at the beginning of the year, and he was totally all over her," Andy said with a laugh. "It was kind of funny, actually, because Liz was staring at Conner and Maria was staring at Conner and Evan was staring at Liz and—"

"Andy!" Jessica said. "You're rambling."

"Yes, yes, I am," Andy deadpanned. "Anyway, I

guess Evan's over Elizabeth now. He and Conner are good friends, so . . ."

"It's weird that she never mentioned him," Jessica said. So obviously Evan didn't mind girls with good personal hygiene. Of course, even if he'd had a chance, the two of them would have looked really weird together.

Jessica glanced up at the stage, where Elizabeth and Conner stood facing each other, creating their own cozy airspace. They certainly looked perfect together. Irritatingly so.

A bittersweet feeling gnawed through her. She shouldn't have come. The thing was, she was happy for Conner and for Elizabeth, but she just couldn't bring that happiness to the surface. Not with everything else pressing down on her.

"God, look at them," Andy grumbled, following Jessica's gaze. "Hey, studmuffin!" he yelled, cupping his hands around his mouth. "Pick up your guitar, not the girl! Let's get the show rolling!"

Conner shot him a withering look, and Jessica laughed.

Oh, well. As long as she was here, she might as well try to relax. She could play the part of the happy-go-lucky Jessica for one night. She could even be nice to this Evan guy, although he seemed like her complete opposite.

It certainly couldn't hurt. At least not any worse than she already hurt.

TIA RAMIREZ

BEEP!

Hey, Angel! It's me. Guess you're not home. Oh, well, just wanted to say hi and that I'm thinking about you. Give me a call.

BEEP!

Hey, it's me again. Miguel said he thought the other line beeped while he was talking with his friend Larry, but he didn't grab it in time. I thought it might have been you trying to reach me. Guess not. Oh, well, give me a call.

BEEP!

Hey! Me again. Wow. You're pulling some long days, huh? Just wanted to tell you some news. Conner has a gig tonight at House of Java. Andy and I are going to spread the word to get a huge crowd there. I figure the more they pack 'em in, the happier the management will be and the more they'll book him. You know me. Anyway . . . so, I won't be home tonight if you call. Okay? So . . . maybe I'll talk to you tomorrow? Hope everything's great. I'll be thinking about you. . . .

CHAPTER 6
Face the Music

Andy leaned back in his chair and watched Conner tune up his guitar. He couldn't believe the size of the crowd. Everyone was there, hanging out in groups of five or six, swilling coffee, and impatiently eyeing the stage as if Elvis himself was going to make an appearance. Squeezed together at their own once big but now rapidly tightening table were Andy, Jessica, Elizabeth, Maria, Ken, and Tia. And he'd had to chase several people out of Evan's empty chair. He wished Evan would hurry up and get back. The drink line must be extra long tonight.

He wondered what Conner thought of the big turnout. Must be nice to look out from the stage and see a room crammed with adoring fans. Hmmm. Maybe Andy should go back to learning the piano? When he was seven, his mother had urged him to take lessons from old Mrs. Kurkowski, who lived down the block.

After six months of listening to complaints from him *and* Mrs. Kurkowski, his mom had finally given in and let him quit. But maybe he should give it another try. At least it would give him something to put on his college applications, and it might even win him a few fans.

Then again, he doubted people would pack the place to hear him pound out a few scales or play such rollicking hits as "Mary Had a Little Lamb" and "Ten Little Indians."

A familiar face appeared in the doorway. Travis Hanson, the Outdoor president himself, was making his way through the crowd, followed by a couple of muscle-bound friends. Even in a pair of jeans and red polo shirt the guy looked ready to perform some awesome physical feat at any moment. Andy wouldn't have been too surprised to see him hurdle the tables or climb the side of a building barehanded. Was it just his pumped-up physique that made him seem so superhuman? Or was it some measure of attitude too?

Travis passed by their table and spotted Andy.

"Hey!" he cried, clapping Andy on the back. "How's it going?"

Andy grinned weakly, desperately trying to inhale again. Travis's friendly little slap seemed to have dislodged a few inner organs. "Fine," Andy finally croaked. "What's up?"

"Just thought we'd check out the show," Travis replied. "A friend of ours told us this guy is really good."

"He is." Andy nodded. "So . . . um, these are my

friends Jessica, Tia, Ken, Maria, and Liz." He gestured around the table. "Guys, this is Travis Hanson. He's president of the Outdoors Club."

Travis nodded to everyone and introduced his two buddies as Mitch and Rob.

"Well, we're going to try to grab some seats at the back," Travis explained as he turned into the crowd. "Good to see ya, Marsden. Nice to meet you all."

"They seemed nice," Maria commented after he'd disappeared into the crowd.

"Yeah," Jessica echoed.

Tia leaned across the table toward Andy. "So tell us about this club, Andy. What's it like?"

Andy lifted his shoulders. "It's cool so far. I've only been to one meeting, though."

"Well, they really seem to like you," Elizabeth said. "I bet you end up having fun after all."

"Yeah," Andy mumbled. "Maybe."

He sighed as he watched Travis, Mitch, and Rob wend their way to a back table. Travis and his buddies seemed nice enough, but he still couldn't help but feel like a nervous little worm around guys like that. They just seemed so strong and confident— heck, they even *walked* confident. Maybe he was only setting himself up for failure in the Outdoors Club. No matter how many hikes he went on, no matter how nice everyone acted toward him, he just couldn't see himself ever truly fitting in with people like that. It could be time to start checking out other extracurriculars. Maybe he could start an indoors club.

"Heads up." A voice suddenly sounded behind him, and a steaming cup of mocha appeared in front of him.

Andy glanced up and saw Evan standing over him with a tray of drinks.

"What's this?" Andy asked.

"Mocha latte," Evan replied. "Plus one lime water for me and"—he reached over and set a large mug in front of Jessica—"a cappuccino for the lady."

"For me?" Jessica asked, raising her eyebrows.

"Yeah. It was taking such a long time getting through the line, I figured I'd go ahead and grab stuff for you guys," he explained. "Here. I got you all some of these too."

He handed Andy and Jessica each a couple of brown-colored, finger-shaped things.

"What are these?" Andy asked, turning them over in his hand.

"You've never had biscotti?" Evan asked.

"No," Andy replied, feeling a little stupid. "They look like dried dog poo."

"They're cookies," Jessica explained with a laugh. "And they're delicious. Thanks a lot, Evan. You really didn't need to do that."

Evan shrugged. "No biggie. I'm afraid I had no idea that the rest of you guys would be here, though. Sorry 'bout that."

"That's okay, Evan," Elizabeth said, grinning. "Some of us are just here for the music."

Wow. What a cool thing to do, Andy thought, taking a sip of mocha. Even Jessica, who had obviously been leery of sitting too close to the guy, seemed impressed by the gesture. Since Elizabeth had grabbed Evan's previous seat, which was closest to the stage and provided the best view of Conner, he now had to take the chair next to Jessica. Andy noticed he wasn't complaining.

Could Evan be checking out the other twin now? Maybe buying her a drink was his way of getting in good with her. Of course, he'd also bought Andy something, and he doubted Evan wanted to hold hands with him later in the evening.

He watched Jessica smile as Evan handed her a spoon and packet of sugar—not exactly the same length as the grin Elizabeth was always giving Conner, but still friendly.

Yep, he thought as he leaned back in his chair. This could be a very interesting evening. Too bad people watching didn't count as an extracurricular activity.

Elizabeth Wakefield

Conner's so totally different when he's playing his music. He seems almost . . . happy. God, he's so talented. Of course he is. That's why they keep booking him. Conner really needs this right now.

Wait. He's playing "Stone Heart."

I lose all train of thought when he plays that.

How did I get this lucky?

Ken Matthews

Just look at Maria. She's so gorgeous tonight in that new red dress. She even smells perfect. It's like, when I'm away from her for a day, all I can think about is that smell. That Maria smell. It's like I'm addicted.

Forget Conner. All I can do is watch Maria.

She has got to be the most incredible girl in the world. How did I get so lucky?

TIA RAMIREZ

THIS IS DISGUSTING. CONNER'S STARING AT ELIZABETH.

ELIZABETH'S EYES ARE
COMPLETELY GLASSY. KEN IS
PRACTICALLY LICKING MARIA'S
FACE. MARIA IS CLUTCHING KEN'S
HAND. EVEN JESSICA KEEPS
SHOOTING LOOKS AT EVAN.

I'M SURROUNDED.

I WONDER WHAT TRENT IS
UP TO. . . .

Andy Marsden

*Damn! What did Evan call these things?
Biscuit somethings? Whatever they are, they
have got to be the best cookies in the world!*

Jessica glanced over at Evan, studying him with
new respect. Obviously she'd been too quick to
judge him. She couldn't believe she'd had such catty
thoughts about someone who would buy a complete
stranger a free drink.

Oh, well. No reason why she couldn't make up
for it now.

"Thanks again for the coffee, Evan," she said,
leaning toward his ear so he could hear her over the
music. "I needed that."

"Good. Glad you like it," he said, bobbing his head to the song.

She found it unnerving that she couldn't see his eyes when he spoke. It made it impossible to read him. Still, she was tired of just sitting there and wanted to talk to someone. To anyone.

"So how did you know I like cappuccino with chocolate sprinkles on top?" she asked. "Am I that obvious?"

"Actually, I didn't know," he said, turning toward her. "The guy behind the counter told me. He said you work here and he knows what you like."

"Oh." Jessica smiled. It was flattering to think he'd gone to the trouble of investigating her preferred drink. Suddenly she cringed, wondering if anything else might have been said about her.

"All right! This song is cool," Evan exclaimed as Conner started up one of his faster tunes.

Jessica watched as Evan drummed his hands on the table and shook his head back and forth to the rhythm. There was something almost cute and engaging about him in spite of his sloppy exterior.

So what if he looked like a cross between Cousin It from the Addams Family and Shaggy on Scooby Doo? She couldn't help but be curious about him. And he was certainly an interesting diversion to the endless pity fest she had been on.

As Conner ended the song, Evan whistled and clapped loudly. "I swear that dude's ready for the H.O.R.D.E. tour," he said.

"Or Lilith Fair," Andy added.

Jessica giggled. Elizabeth had been right. Jessica was having an okay time. Here, surrounded by old and new buddies, Will seemed like a distant memory.

Evan lifted his glass of sparkling water to his mouth, tilted it, and downed one-third of the contents instantly. Jessica watched the up-and-down motion of his Adam's apple and followed the square line of his jaw. She wondered what he'd look like with a decent haircut and close shave.

He set his glass back on the table and turned toward her. "Are you staring at me?" he asked, grinning.

"What?" Jessica could feel her cheeks reddening. "N-No. I was just wondering . . . about your drink. You're the only one not having coffee tonight. Got anything against caffeine?"

"No," he replied. "I just can't bring myself to order imported coffees. It bothers me to think that all those beans were picked by some poor South American peasant who only gets paid pennies a day."

"God, you make it sound so awful. I thought Juan Valdez and his donkey were just a logo," she said, laughing.

Evan sighed. "Yeah, that's just the sort of viewpoint I'd expect from someone who's probably never gotten a single blister or even broken a nail doing hard labor."

Jessica's mouth dropped open in shock. Again she tried to get a glimpse of Evan's eyes to see if he

81

was serious or only teasing, but she couldn't see a thing through his tangled bangs. Judging from his set jaw, though, he'd meant what he said.

"It was just a joke," she said softly. "What makes you think you can tell me off like that? You don't even know me."

For a moment Evan said nothing. Then a smile slowly crept across the exposed half of his face. "You're right," he said, nodding. "I don't. So . . . enlighten me. Tell me all about yourself."

Jessica squinted at him. Was he toying with her? Or did he actually want to know? It was impossible to tell with this guy.

"Okay . . . ," she replied warily. "Like what?"

He shrugged slightly. "Tell me what you do in your spare time."

She glanced around at the others at the table. They were all looking at her sympathetically. Great. Just what she needed. She came here to forget her troubles, not become the butt of jokes.

Still, it was a pretty tame question. What did she have to lose? She'd show this slacker she had nothing to fear.

"Well, I do lots of things," she began. "Acting, dancing, cheerleading . . ."

Evan gave a slight snort, stopping her short.

"What?" she asked indignantly. "What's wrong?"

"Nothing," he said, shrugging slightly. "Actually, we're not all that different. See, I'm a bit of a cheerleader myself."

Jessica frowned. What was he talking about?

"I'm involved in lots of these activist organizations—you know, Amnesty International, Greenpeace, PETA. So, instead of hollering my lungs out for a football team, I march on the Capitol and demand rights for migrant workers. And instead of turning flips and cartwheels because some guy carried a ball past a painted line, I attend rallies on human-rights issues in Tibet. But really, it's not all *that* different."

Jessica could feel her cheeks flare up like torches. She heard Andy stifling a chuckle. Everyone else was careful not to look at her.

What was with this guy? Was he some nutcase who got off on embarrassing people as a hobby? How dare he mock her like that?

She pushed away her complimentary drink and turned her full attention to Conner. No way would she give this joker the time of day anymore.

And from now on she was trusting her instincts.

Conner McDermott

When I was three years old, my dad kept promising that when summer rolled around, he'd take me to Disneyland. I was so psyched. My buddy Tommy Puett had been there, and all he could talk about were the rides and the cotton candy and the big Mickey Mouse who would shake your hand if you weren't shy. I told everyone my dad was taking me, and because I wouldn't stop asking if today was the day, my dad even marked a date on the calendar when we would go.

Every day my mom helped me put a big

x through the date to mark how close we were getting, and I even started practicing handshakes with my stuffed Mickey doll. It seemed like the day would never arrive.

It never did. Three weeks before I "x'ed" my way to the date circled in red, my dad left without saying good-bye.

So unlike my dad, I make it a point to always keep my promises. I may have a spotty record for picking up and dumping girls at the drop of the hat, but I've never, ever told them things I didn't mean.

Too bad Tia wasn't taught the same lesson about promises. I guess that's what you get for having a solid family life.

CHAPTER 7

Totally Distracting

Jessica opened up the top of House of Java's sleek metal espresso maker, took out the basket of used grounds, and dumped them into the waste bin. In order to dislodge the more stubborn bits of residue without getting her hands dirty, she had to slam the container against the side of the can. And slam it. And slam it. And slam it.

The violence of the motion and the harshness of the noise was somehow therapeutic. Jessica imagined herself whacking a heavy metal object against a certain guy's swelled and monstrously hairy head.

Coming into work at House of Java that afternoon felt like returning to the scene of a crime. She couldn't push aside the memory of how Evan had embarrassed her.

"Who does that guy think he is?" she muttered as she continued banging away. "Thinks he can sum me up as a brainless bimbo after talking to me for two minutes? Jerk! First he makes me think he's all nice by buying me a drink, then he goes off on me for making a stupid joke. I was *only being friendly!*"

She punctuated each of those final words with a brutal knock against the trash can.

"Everything all right?" Ally called, poking her head out of the office.

"Um . . . yeah. Fine," Jessica replied. "I was just emptying the old grounds. You know how they can stick."

Ally nodded and disappeared back through the doorway.

You're losing it, Wakefield, Jessica scolded herself as she refilled the receptacle with fresh grounds. She had to get a grip soon; otherwise she'd end up scaring off customers or accidentally scalding them as she threw stuff around.

If only she didn't have to work tonight. She could be in her own bed, reading magazines, or drowning her psyche in some mopey TV drama. But no. Instead she had to wrangle with these thoughts for an entire four-hour shift. Maybe she should just fake being sick and go back home.

An ironic smile crept over Jessica's face. She knew she'd spent enough time moping around the house these past few days. Actually, that was the one and only good thing about the whole Evan incident: It had definitely taken her mind off Will. At least for today.

The door chimes sounded, and Jessica could see the silhouette of a customer outlined against the sunlit glass door.

So the evening rush begins, she told herself.

Hopefully it would be nice and psychotically busy. Totally distracting.

As soon as the figure stepped up toward the counter, Jessica knew distraction would be no problem. It was a guy. The kind of guy who brought a blush to Jessica's face just by looking at her.

He was tall, with lean muscles, and his hair was wet and slicked back from his forehead, as if he'd just come in from the ocean. His skin was a deep olive color, and he had a perfectly square jaw. But his eyes were the feature that really caught her attention. They were an amazing dark blue, and they were staring right at her.

Jessica powered up her grin to full voltage. "Hi," she said. "Can I get you anything?" *Anything at all?* she added silently.

"Hey, Jessica," the guy replied with a slight smirk.

Jessica could feel her grin falter. She was sure she'd never met this guy.

He laughed, and a vaguely unsettling feeling gripped Jessica's stomach. "It's Evan. From last night. Remember?" he said, placing one hand on his chest. "Man! And I thought that whole thing about blondes being dumb was just a lousy stereotype."

Evan? The Evan? Jessica's brain locked up, refusing to process something so incredibly illogical.

She squinted at him. There *was* something about his angular jawline that seemed familiar. And those lean, muscular legs. And that laugh . . .

Her stomach was turning as if it had been shoved into a blender. It *was* him. But how? How could this gorgeous person be even the same species as the thing that insulted her here just last night?

"Right," she said, slowly regaining her cool. "Well, I'm just tired from the after-school coffee stampede. Real busy today. In fact, take a look." She held up her right hand and wiggled her first two fingers. "Blisters—from twisting the steamer knob on the cappuccino machine for two hours straight. Sort of blows your theory about me, huh?"

Evan smiled—a genuinely friendly-looking smile that made his eyes twinkle like onyx. Jessica fought down the now fluttery sensation in her stomach.

So what if he was cute? He'd just called her a dumb blonde to her face.

"I'm sure taking orders from privileged high-school kids can get pretty oppressive, huh?" he said, leaning against the counter.

"Sometimes," she replied, trying not to smile as she grabbed a rag to wipe down the counter. "But I just tell them to get a real life. You know, march to Sacramento to protest something or at least humiliate those you feel might be more shallow and naive than you are." She shoved the rag toward his arms so he'd have to move out of her personal space.

Evan's grin widened as he backed up slightly. "Hey, I never said you were shallow," he said.

"No." Jessica raised her chin, scrubbing even harder. "But you implied it."

"Well, if it makes you feel better, I don't think you're shallow." His eyes drooped in a sort of apologetic expression.

"Good," Jessica said, feeling herself thaw out slightly.

"Maybe a little clueless, but not shallow," he added.

"Clueless!"

"Yeah." He was smiling again. "As in ignorant. Misinformed. I didn't mean the Alicia Silverstone movie."

Jessica shot him an icy glare. "Oh, really? I'm surprised you even know who Alicia Silverstone is. I would have thought you boycotted all movie theaters because they serve popcorn instead of granola bars."

"Actually, I like popcorn," he said. "It's those hot dogs under the heat lamps I object to. It's totally cruel."

"Cruel to who?" Jessica asked. "The animals they make them out of or the poor slobs who eat them?"

"Both!"

Jessica stared at him for a moment, holding her breath, and he stared right back. There was a giggle working its way up her throat, and suddenly she couldn't take it anymore. She burst out laughing at the exact same moment that Evan lost it too.

Evan shook his head as his laughter subsided. "Are

we going to stop sounding like idiots now?" he asked. All traces of a smirk had disappeared, and there was something new behind his gaze. Something closely resembling . . . respect?

"I know I am, but I'm not sure if you're capable," Jessica said.

Evan grinned and opened his mouth to say something, but at that moment the chimes sounded again, and Elizabeth suddenly burst through the door. "Jessica!" she shouted, racing up to the counter. "You won't believe what happened."

"What?" Jessica's forehead crinkled up with worry. "You're all red, Liz."

"I just ran over from the mall," Elizabeth answered.

Jessica poured a glass of water for Elizabeth and threw in an extra one for Evan. She figured Elizabeth probably didn't recognize him and was just about to slyly drop his name into the conversation when Elizabeth turned to him and said, "Hey, Ev."

"Hey, Liz," he replied.

Jessica was shocked. Maybe Elizabeth had seen him with his hair off his face before. Or maybe she was just able to see beyond hairstyles—or at least *through* them.

"So . . . aren't you going to ask me what I was doing at the mall?" Elizabeth said excitedly.

"Okay. What were you doing there?" Jessica asked.

Elizabeth raised her glass in a toasting gesture and grinned widely. "I got a job!" she announced giddily.

"Really? That's great!" Jessica said. "Doing what?"

"I'm going to work at the Sedona counter."

"No way!" Jessica exclaimed. "*You're* going to sell *makeup?*"

Elizabeth's face fell. "Yeah. Why not?"

"Only because it furthers the efforts of the mass media to get us to buy into megacorporations' view of beauty," Evan said. "Only because people are bilked out of their hard-earned money to buy chemical compounds that dozens of animals probably had to give up their lives for."

"Blah, blah, blah," Elizabeth said, eliciting a laugh from Evan.

Weird, Jessica thought. Apparently her sister already knew how to handle the guy.

"I don't care what Mr. Greenpeace thinks," Elizabeth said, raising her chin. "I'm going to make ridiculous amounts of money on commissions, most of which I'll be able to save up for college."

"Exactly," Jessica said, glancing at Evan. "You can't be anti–higher education."

"Don't even get me started," Evan said.

Jessica wasn't about to. "We should go out and celebrate," she told her sister. "How about we meet up at the Riot later on tonight?"

"It'll be an Eliza-palooza," Elizabeth deadpanned.

"I'm there," Evan said, his deep blue eyes locking onto Jessica's.

Just like the night before, Jessica could feel her cheeks ripen—only this time in a good way.

Evan might be incredibly irritating, but he definitely had potential.

"Hanson residence!" the female voice squawked from the other end of the line. There was no mistaking who that hundred-decibel greeting came from.

"Hello, Six?" Andy said, strumming his index finger on the phone cord. "This is Andy Marsden. You know, the fresh meat for the Outdoors Club."

"*An*-dee!"

Andy couldn't remember when anyone had ever given him such an enthusiastic greeting. So enthusiastic, he had to hold the phone away from his ear.

"Of course, I remember you. How's it going?" she said.

"I'm cool. Thanks," he replied, shifting uncomfortably in his desk chair. Her friendliness helped lessen his nervousness somewhat, but he still couldn't shake the nagging sensation that he was about to embarrass himself royally. This whole calling-the-shots type of stuff was totally new to him. He was never the one doing the organizing of things. Instead he usually just tagged along on other people's careful planning.

"So anyway," he went on, forcing some conviction

94

into his voice. Six obviously thought he was cool, so why couldn't he act it? "A friend of mine just got a new job, and we're all going to meet at the Riot to congratulate her and make her buy us all expensive drinks. You still interested in going tonight?"

"Sure! Why wouldn't I be?"

Andy breathed a sigh of relief. "Oh, I don't know. Because it's a cramped, dimly lit, smoky cave with ear-mangling music and hardly any chairs. But don't worry—it'll be a great crowd tonight. I'm sure you'll have fun."

"I'm sure I will," she said, lowering her voice to a normal level.

"Great. Well, then. Uh . . . what time should I pick you up?" Andy asked. Very confident . . . for an eighth grader.

At least Six didn't seem to notice his lameness. "Doesn't matter," she said brightly. "Hey! Have you had dinner yet?"

"Uh . . . no. Why?"

"I don't know. I just thought maybe we could, you know, go grab some food beforehand," she said. "Then we could actually hear each other talk some before we go to the noisy club."

"Okay. Yeah," he replied, nodding into the receiver. His mouth had gone completely dry, so he cleared his throat noisily. "We'll . . . talk."

Six giggled. "Good! How about you come get me around seven?"

"No problem," he said. "See you at seven, Six."

Andy hung up the phone and was surprised to feel a grin lighting his face. The girl was so psyched to be with him. Maybe this was just what he needed. A major ego boost in the form of a loud yet cool new friend.

Maybe now his friends would take him seriously.

Who knew? Maybe he'd start taking himself seriously.

Jessica smoothed the skirt of her baby blue peasant dress and turned sideways to study herself in the wall mirror.

There was something different about her today. Jessica couldn't quite put her finger on it. Her reflection looked exactly the same as she'd always remembered, only her features seemed somehow . . . softer? Maybe it was just the lighting in her new bedroom. Or maybe it was simply hunger since she barely touched the leftover tuna casserole that was waiting for her after her work shift. Whatever it was, she couldn't decide if she liked the change or not.

"Wow, Jess. You look great," Elizabeth said as she stood in the doorway to Jessica's bedroom. "Where'd you get that dress?"

"At the mall last week. I was saving it to wow Will with sometime, but . . ." She frowned at her reflection, letting her words taper off. She didn't want to feel sorry for herself. Not anymore.

"His loss," Elizabeth said, sitting on the edge of Jessica's bed. "So am I wrong in thinking you've chosen to wear this tonight in order to make Evan Plummer speechless?"

Jessica shrugged slightly and continued to fiddle with her sleeves. No sense trying to deny it. Her twin knew her all too well. But Jessica didn't exactly want to admit it aloud either. She wasn't exactly sure she could focus on anyone else so soon after Will. But that was what she had always done, right? If it didn't work out with one guy, move right on to the next.

It was like the Jessica Wakefield creed.

But as far as she wanted the world to know, she was just going out to help her sister celebrate her new job. Nothing more. And if she happened to snag Evan's interest along the way, well, that was just coincidence.

"Uh-huh," Elizabeth answered for her. "I thought so. Good—it's nice to see you in flaunt-it mode again. That means you're on the road to recovery. Before you know it, Will Simmons will be just another number on the football team."

I hope so, Jessica thought. She'd already wasted too much of the school year on that guy. But Elizabeth was right. Jessica was definitely shaking him off. In fact, ever since she met Evan, Will hadn't entered her mind much at all. And when he did, it wasn't accompanied by those sharp, sledgehammer blows to her heart. Well, not *always,* at least.

"Speaking of roads to recovery," Jessica said to Elizabeth's reflection, "how did Mom and Dad react when you told them about the new job?"

"Are you kidding? They were psyched beyond belief," she said. "Only, they were also a little surprised to hear I'll be selling makeup. Just like you were." Her smile slowly faded.

Jessica spun around to face her. "Come on! You said yourself you were going to make millions, and you will. Just look at you." She turned and gestured toward Elizabeth's silk chemise and black slacks ensemble. With her hair swept up in a sleek French twist, she seemed much older and sophisticated than seventeen.

"Whatever," Elizabeth said, standing up. She leaned in to the mirror and tucked a stray hair behind her ear. "You're the one who's dressed to kill. I'll have to strip to get any attention. Evan's seriously in for it. I almost feel bad for the guy."

"Please!" Jessica protested, but she smiled at her reflection. "It's not like he's been falling at my feet so far. I'm not even totally sure I like him."

She just needed a distraction. Someone who wasn't Will. And if anyone was Will Simmons's polar opposite, it was Evan.

Reaching up, she gently pulled the elastic sleeves of her dress down off her shoulders for a more provocative look. Then, pivoting back and forth and studying the effect, she changed her mind and lifted them back up.

"Okay," she said, turning to face Elizabeth. "I'm ready."

Elizabeth rolled her eyes. "Those sleeves will be back down five seconds after you get there," she said, strolling out of the room.

Jessica said nothing as she turned off the light and followed her sister. After all, the girl was probably right.

```
Dear Tia,
  I miss you too. I really do. I
think about you a lot, only I don't
really have that much time to think
after classes and training and work
and
```

"No," Angel muttered, highlighting his entire letter and erasing it with the push of the delete button.

It was just too whiny. He hadn't had a chance to write Tia in days, and now that he could, he certainly didn't want to unload all his stress on her.

Try again.

```
Dear Tia,
  In your e-mail last Monday you
asked about my Christmas vacation. As
far as I know, I'll have the last two
```

```
weeks of December off. In your letter
on Tuesday you asked me if I got your
package. Yes, I did. Thanks! You
really shouldn't have, baby. In your
letter on Wednesday
```

"No way," he said, wiping out the screen again. What was that? A letter or a laundry list? No sense calling attention to the fact that he'd been an awful boyfriend lately.

All right. One more time . . .

```
Dear Tia,
   Hey, baby! How are you? Things are
okay here. I've met some cool people
in the dorm. This one guy, Cody, is
totally nuts! Last night we went and
grabbed some pizza down the street,
and while we were there, he dared me
to
```

"What the hell am I doing?" Angel let his head drop into his hands. No way could he tell her about that. It was one thing to spare her all the stress in his life. But it would almost be worse to tell her about all the fun he was having.

Still, he wanted to share part of his life with her—something besides computer algorithms or boring professors or putrid cafeteria food. He wanted to somehow bring her closer to him.

"There's only one way to do that," he muttered, jumping up from his desk. He walked over to his closet and pulled down his green nylon satchel. He was going to go see her.

Why hadn't he thought of it before? He definitely had the money after working extra shifts at the bookstore for his coworker Corrine while she pledged some sorority. Plus he could cash in on the favor and get the weekend off.

Angel tossed a few changes of clothes, his shaving kit, and his computer-science textbook into his bag. Just having a plan of action made him feel completely better. Forget phone calls and letters—it was time to communicate with Tia in person.

He rummaged through his desk drawer for Corrine's number and picked up his phone. *Wait a sec,* he thought, setting it back down. *Maybe I should check with Tia first and make sure it's all right.*

But it was too late. Tia would probably be out at the Riot by now, and he didn't want to call at curfew time and risk waking up her parents. Nah, he'd just head out early tomorrow morning without calling. Besides, what was she going to say? No?

Man, I can't wait to see her, he thought, picking up the phone again. *She's going to be so surprised!*

Elizabeth Wakefield

It really bothers me that some people are surprised by my new job. What? Do they think only heavily painted up bimbos can sell makeup? I mean, forgive me if I don't look like Pamela Anderson-Lee-Lee-Anderson or whatever the heck her name is now. I can push cosmetics as well as the next girl. Even better.

I guess I shouldn't be too surprised that they're surprised. A year ago I wouldn't have even considered working there. I would have thought it was shallow. And I probably would have jumped right in and agreed with Evan about commercialism and how hung up society is on beauty. But I guess I've changed.

Don't get me wrong—I haven't

turned into a Lila Fowler clone who spends all her time at the mall or in front of her dresser mirror. But I have learned to take things less seriously.

Let's face it—makeup is fun and harmless. Being a feminist doesn't mean you can't be feminine. It's that kind of thinking that makes people shallow, not their cosmetics.

Okay. I realize you can't make real problems disappear with a dab of blusher and lipstick. I'm not saying makeup is the answer. But it's not the force of evil some people make it out to be either.

And right now it's the best way I have of making money for college. So what's so wrong with that?

"So before my dad and I set up the tent, it was my job to clear away all the rocks. I swear I went over that space four times and picked up anything the size of a pebble. But then later that night, when I finally crawled into my sleeping bag, there was this boulder the size of a loaf of bread right under my back." Andy held out his hands to estimate the size.

"How'd you miss that?" Six asked, her eyes wide and her cheeseburger suspended midway to her mouth. Andy loved the way she held on to every word of the story, as if he were some wartime hero telling tales.

"I had no idea," Andy replied. "And I barely slept. But sure enough, when we rolled up the tent the next day, there was this huge mound right where I'd been lying."

"Wait," Six said. "Tell me it wasn't a rock."

Andy gave her his best deadpan expression. "It was a turtle."

Six's sputtering laughter echoed throughout First and Ten, causing some of the diners at nearby tables to turn and stare. Andy felt like Jay Leno. He hadn't gotten so many great laughs in ages.

There was just something about Six that put him at ease. Usually he took on the role of "lovable side-kick" to all his drama-queen buddies, but with Six he truly felt like he was the center of attention. It was probably because of the age difference. When Andy was a sophomore, he used to think the seniors were so cool, they could do no wrong.

"You slept on a turtle all night?" Six blurted out. "Poor thing."

Andy nodded. "No kidding. My back was sore for two weeks."

"I meant the turtle!" she exclaimed, pelting him with a balled-up napkin that ricocheted into the middle of the restaurant.

"Yeah, yeah. Take *his* side," Andy said, pretending to rub his arm where the napkin had hit him.

Their waiter strode up to the table, grabbing the napkin from the floor. "Do you guys need anything else tonight?" he asked, an edge of impatience in his voice.

Andy looked at his watch. It was already close to nine. He couldn't believe they'd sat there talking for that long. "Uh . . . no. We're fine. Thanks," he said.

The waiter gave a slight nod and moved on to another table. *Oo-kay,* Andy thought. *Guess someone's worried he won't make enough tips tonight.*

He picked up his double-decker hamburger,

106

which had already grown cold. "So shut me up already," he said, grinning at Six. "I've been blabbing so much, I haven't had a chance to eat my food. It's your turn."

Six wrinkled up her nose. "What do you want to know?"

"Okay. I'll start off with a really tough question." Andy lowered his brows and mimicked the dramatic baritone of his guidance counselor. "Tell me, young lady, what do you want to do after graduation?"

"That's easy!" she said, chewing a mouthful of food. "I've had that planned out since, like, fourth grade."

"Really?" Andy asked, incredulous. "What are you gonna do?"

"I'm going to be an anthropologist, just like my dad," she replied. "I'll get my degree from either San Diego or the University of Arizona—I haven't decided yet. Then I'll spend my days traveling to exotic places, digging up fossils and artifacts, piecing together human history, and getting a killer tan." She flashed him a grin.

"Wow," Andy said, marveling at the conviction behind her voice. "That simple, huh?"

"No. Not really," Six said, taking a sip of her root beer. "It's, like, *crazy* amounts of schoolwork and training. Plus my dad had to publish a lot of stuff to get people to respect him."

"Why don't you use Coach Riley as one of your

studies?" he suggested. "I always wondered if the guy might be the missing link."

Six laughed again, and there was an audible sigh from the table behind her. She covered her mouth with her hand. "Stop!" she gasped. "They're going to, like, stone me or something."

"Don't worry," Andy said, taking a huge bite of his burger. "I'll protect you."

Six's eyes sparkled as she dug into her own food, but Andy wasn't kidding. He was having way too good a time to lose his date to a medieval death.

Jessica followed Elizabeth into the muggy darkness of the Riot, sleeves pulled back down onto her arms. There was already a sizable crowd. People stood clustered at the tables and bars, and the rotating lights above the dance floor bounced off a sea of gyrating arms and legs. Jessica couldn't wait to hit the dance floor.

For the first time in a long while she felt very "on." She could almost feel the heads turning to check her out as she made her way toward the back seating area. The pulsating sounds of the song the DJ was spinning seemed like her very own background theme, making her walk in time to the rhythm. Tonight had the potential to be big. She could literally feel it.

"There they are!" Elizabeth shouted over the music, pointing to a table in the corner. Jessica looked up and spotted Conner straddling one of the metal chairs as if it were a Harley-Davidson.

I wonder if Evan is here yet, Jessica thought, nervously scanning the group at the table.

"Hey! Congrats, girl!" Tia ran up and hooked an arm around Elizabeth's neck as she and Jessica made their way to the table. "I hope this means you'll be giving me a discount."

"You bet," Elizabeth replied.

"Hey," Conner said, standing and pulling Elizabeth close. He whispered something in Elizabeth's ear, and Elizabeth smiled blissfully.

Jessica glanced around, looking for Evan, but came up empty. Ken and Maria waved from the opposite end of the table. A couple of Ken's football buddies hovered over him, noisily recounting some sports story, while Maria talked animatedly to some slouchy skater dude. There was no sign of the hottie Jessica had encountered at HOJ that afternoon.

Maybe he'd changed his mind about coming. Or maybe he'd decided she was too clueless to associate with after all. Jessica felt her shoulders start to droop as her good mood went into a decline.

So much for distraction.

"Hey, Jess," Conner said, turning his face away from Elizabeth long enough to greet her.

"Hey," Jessica responded, planting her hands on the back of an empty chair. She shot for a nonchalant look. "So . . . uh . . . is everyone here?"

Conner shook his head. "Not quite."

"Oh? Who else is coming?" Jessica asked, twisting her left foot back and forth.

"Marsden isn't here yet," Conner said, grabbing a pretzel from the table and popping it into his mouth. The boy, as always, was totally oblivious. Not that Jessica thought that was a bad thing in this particular situation.

"Oh. Right."

Did that mean Evan wasn't planning on showing at all? Or did Conner even know Evan had included himself? She hoped he turned up soon. Before this giddy self-confidence dissipated completely.

Elizabeth broke away from Conner and leaned her chin on Jessica's shoulder. "What's wrong?" she whispered. "You look sort of jittery."

"I'm fine," Jessica muttered, craning her neck to see past Elizabeth toward the front door.

"Uh-huh." Elizabeth grinned knowingly. "Well, if you're looking for Evan, he's right over there."

"Where?" Jessica asked, freezing in place.

"Right there," Elizabeth said, lifting her chin slightly. "Talking to Maria."

What?

Jessica rescrutinized the grungy guy her eyes had passed over earlier. Sure enough, there were the toned legs poking out from under a pair of ripped Bermuda shorts and a familiar square jawline peeking out from under his ratty hair as he spoke.

Evan number one, aka Mr. Hyde, was back.

Jessica had the distinct sensation she was losing her grasp of reality—or at least her twenty-twenty vision.

Evan looked up at her and waved, pushing his hair back from his face and giving her a quick glimpse of Evan number two. He was still cute under there. And funny, and smart, and challenging. Plus he was obviously excited to see her, so Jessica forced a smile.

She just couldn't figure out why she suddenly felt like she wanted to be anywhere but here.

"Not me. Sorry. I hate camping." Tia twisted around in her seat to face Six, her voice practically shouting so she could be heard over the Riot's sound system. "Me and my four smelly brothers crammed together in a tiny tent. No running water. No hair dryer. Food out of a can. That's more like capital punishment than a vacation. Besides, every time we tried it, we would end up in a freak hailstorm or something."

Six laughed heartily, her long braid swinging like a pendulum over the back of her chair. "Oh, well. At least you didn't end up sleeping on a turtle like Andy."

Tia, Conner, and Elizabeth stared at Andy questioningly.

"Long story," Andy said, smirking. "I'll tell you

some other time." He leaned back against his chair, disengaging himself from the conversation. It was more fun watching Six being surrounded by his friends, answering all their questions in that high-powered voice of hers. Since they'd arrived at the Riot, she'd been accepted immediately. And he could tell she loved every minute of it.

"So, I have to ask." Tia turned back toward Six and rested her chin in her hand. "What's the story behind your name?"

"You know, I think we should give that subject a rest," Andy said, raising a hand to object. "I mean, just because she happens to have the same last name as a has-been teenybopper band doesn't give us the right to tease her."

Six shook her head, chuckling.

Tia scowled. "I meant her *first* name, moron!"

"Oh, I see." Andy flashed a grin. "That's okay, then."

Six nudged Tia's shoulder. "God! Is he, like, *ever* serious?"

"No," Tia, Conner, and Elizabeth answered in unison.

"Just ignore him," Elizabeth said with a wave of her hand. Andy felt a blush rise to his face. He knew Elizabeth was kidding, but she had no idea how close to home she'd hit. Until he started hanging out with Six, he'd felt ignored by everyone.

"So what were you going to tell us about your name?" Elizabeth continued.

"Okay, well, I'm the last of six kids . . . ," Six began.

"She's really sweet." Maria leaned over and whispered into Andy's ear. "What a voice! I swear she should be onstage. Were we that superperky when we were sophomores?"

"Probably," he replied. "At least, I'm sure you were."

Maria smirked. "Well, I like her. She's totally comfortable in a crowd full of strangers."

Andy smiled to himself. Usually he was the one who felt like a hanger-on—being pegged as "Conner's friend Andy" or "Tia Ramirez's sidekick." Now here was someone who could be dubbed "Andy's friend Six."

"Hey, Andy." Six put her hand on his arm, breaking him out of his thoughts. "I've gotta get home soon."

"Really?" Andy asked.

"Yeah," she said with an apologetic shrug. "I have to work early tomorrow at Mom's store. Sorry to be so lame."

"No big deal," he replied. "I should probably get home early too so I can start saving energy for that big hike on Sunday."

"Don't forget." She reached up and tapped the tip of his nose with her index finger. "You promised to come by the shop tomorrow and get some gear."

"I'll be there."

Andy stood and waited for Six as she went

around the table, saying good-bye to everyone.

"Tell Andy to bring you back sometime," Tia said.

Andy smiled. Apparently his new climbing partner passed inspection.

"Um, Andy? Can I talk with you for a sec?"

He looked over and saw Elizabeth standing next to him, her forehead creased as she glanced at Six. "Over here," Elizabeth said, gesturing over her shoulder.

Andy's stomach gave a little squeeze as he stood up. What was going on?

"What's up?" he asked.

Elizabeth grabbed his upper arm and steered him away from the table. "When you called me to tell me you were bringing Six tonight, didn't you say you were just friends?" she whispered as soon as they were out of earshot.

"Yeah, that's what I said." Andy stared at Elizabeth quizzically.

"Well, did it happen to escape your attention that she has a major crush on you?" Elizabeth asked. "She's been shooting you lovey-dovey looks all night."

Andy cracked up. "What? No way!"

"Yeah, way," Elizabeth insisted, crossing her arms over her chest in a classic "listen-to-me-you-moron" gesture. "I think she thinks this is a date."

"She does not." He shook his head. "She's just a cool girl. We're friends, that's all."

Elizabeth squinted at him uncertainly. "I still think you should watch out. You have this way of making people feel superimportant to you right off the bat, and Six might be taking that the wrong way."

"Yeah, right," Andy said, laughing. "I'm just way too nice. That's why I'm always fighting women off with a big stick."

Elizabeth laughed but recovered quickly. "I'm serious, Andy," she said, glancing past him to the table. "Have you ever stopped to consider that Six might think this is more than a new *friendship?*"

Andy's heart gave a little thud of apprehension, but he tried to mask it. "You know, Liz, I appreciate you looking out for me and all, but you're nuts. Totally and absolutely insane."

Elizabeth sighed wearily. "Look. Just be careful, okay?"

"Whatever." He rolled his eyes and chuckled to himself.

As Elizabeth walked back to the table, Andy looked over at Six, who was saying good-bye to Jessica. Her eyes were wide and glittery, and she nodded briskly at everything Jessica was saying.

He let himself relax slightly. Six was obviously just psyched about hanging out with seniors. That was all.

Just as that thought was escaping his mind, Six looked over and caught him staring at her. She blushed and gave him a soft smile. It was an expression he hadn't seen on her face since they'd met.

A possibly intimate expression. Possibly because Andy had never experienced an intimate anything before.

He lifted his hand in a slight wave, pushed the thought aside, and swallowed hard. He was right in the first place. Elizabeth couldn't be more wrong about Six.

Could she?

Jessica looked out at the dance floor and fiddled absently with the front tie string of her dress. Her sleeves were back up on her shoulders now, and her go-get-'em attitude had completely disappeared into the heavy air of the club.

She was only pretending to watch the dancers. In reality she was watching Evan out of the corner of her eye and listening to him debate the ethics of the music industry with Conner.

Every time she looked at him, she got a strange, leaden feeling in the pit of her stomach. She wasn't sure if she was paying enough attention to him. Or too much. Or if he even cared. Jessica had never been so confused around a guy before. She was just hoping someone else would get tired soon and bring her home.

"I wish I had your optimism, man," Evan was saying to Conner. "But if you don't want to strap on your dancing shoes and join a boy band, I don't think the business will come calling. They aren't looking for talent. They're looking for *marketability*."

Jessica rolled her eyes. Okay. That cynicism thing could get grating. At least Will was simple. At least he—

She pressed her lips together as if that could stop her inner voice. Suddenly she felt sweat prickling at the back of her neck. *Is this place always so hot?* she wondered as her elbow was jostled by a huge guy with an awful nose ring. *Or this crowded?*

"Lighten up, Plummer," Conner said, shifting in his seat. "All those backstreet, new-kids, five-alive, in-stink wuss groups die eventually."

"Yeah," Evan said with a snort. He fished the lime out of his glass of water and sucked on the rind. "But you'll be lucky if the next trend is toward talented men-with-guitars and not whiny women, gangsta rap, flashy country, or gyrating Latinos."

Jessica sighed and leaned forward, trying to ignore her jittery nerves. "Can you guys stop talking industry politics for five seconds?" she asked, pushing her hands into her hair. "We're here for Liz, remember?"

"Thank you!" Elizabeth stood and grabbed Conner's hand, pulling him to his feet. "Enough talk. Let's dance."

"Yeah," said Maria, pushing away from the table and grinning at Ken. "Let's go, Matthews."

Ken raised his eyebrows. "Can't deny a request like that."

The two couples headed toward the dance floor and were immediately swallowed up by the hip-hopping crowd.

Jessica felt a twinge of panic. She didn't mean for *that* to happen. Suddenly she was alone with Evan at a table for ten.

Completely conspicuous.

She could just imagine how she would feel if Will and Melissa walked in right now. She'd probably just spontaneously combust from embarrassment. They'd definitely assume she and Evan were here together, and Jessica would never live it down. Following up the fabulous Will Simmons with the most sarcastic, unkempt politico at SVH? She'd be toast.

Jessica immediately started glancing around for Tia, who was off getting a pitcher of Coke, but looking over her shoulders felt even more obvious. She sank down lower in her chair, her left foot tapping in double time to the music.

Evan turned toward her and lifted one side of his mouth in a half smile. "So," he said. "Do you like this song?"

"Oh, yeah! It's great!" Jessica exclaimed—a bit too emphatically. She knew he was going to start in on her about Will Smith being too . . . successful or something.

Predictably enough, Evan smirked and took a deep breath.

Here it comes. . . .

He got up from his chair and held out his hand. "So, you want to dance?"

Jessica's heart hit the floor.

That she wasn't prepared for.

As Evan led Jessica out onto the dance floor moments later, she felt like she was about to burst out of her skin. She felt like everyone in the room was watching her. Why was she so tense? It was one dance. They'd get it over with, and she'd be fine. Who cared what everyone thought anyway?

Of course, the second they found even five inches of space to stand in, the hip-hop song came to an abrupt stop and a slow ballad suddenly crackled through the speakers.

Sweat broke out on Jessica's palms. Okay, so it was one *slow* dance.

Evan smiled and pulled her into his arms. Jessica instantly froze up, her mind a clutter of thoughts and emotions. She felt awkward, tense, sad, nostalgic, and stupid all at once. She should have been here with Will. But she knew she should also freeze the jerk out of her mind. She wanted to get on with her life and be the confident person she'd felt like when she'd walked in that night. But for some reason, at that moment, all she felt was small.

The only thought that came through loud and clear was that she didn't want to be dancing with Evan. Not now.

119

Relax, she told herself, easing her arms around him. *It's just a dance.*

But she couldn't do it. Something just didn't feel right. His body felt warm and strong, and he smelled pleasant enough—a mixture of sea salt and tanning lotion. And yet something in her mind kept telling her it was all wrong.

As they slowly swayed around in a circle, a crowd of onlookers came into Jessica's view. There was Elizabeth, sitting back at their table, smiling at her. There was Tia, making her way back with the new pitcher. And there, standing off to the side, stood Lila Fowler and Cherie Reese.

Jessica suddenly felt like she was standing in a spotlight. Were they looking at her? Was she the one they were nudging each other and whispering about? What were they saying?

Were they going to tell Will?

A new coating of perspiration erupted onto her skin. And millions of eyes from all directions appeared to be fixed right on her.

"Wait!" she blurted out, breaking out of Evan's arms.

"What's wrong?" he asked, pushing aside his hair. His eyes were revealed—wide and worried looking. "Are you okay?"

"N-No. I . . ." She began backing away. "I just don't feel well all of a sudden. I have to . . . go to the bathroom." She turned and raced off into the crowd, maiming about a dozen innocent feet as she went.

Jessica burst into the bathroom and quickly shut the door behind her. Ignoring the couple of goth smokers in the corner, she walked over to the sink, grasping the sides of the basin. Soon the dizziness abated and her heartbeat slackened. Only then did she confront her image in the mirror.

"What's wrong with you?" she whispered to herself. "Are you so superficial that you can't even have one dance with a guy because you're too worried about what people think?"

Her reflection simply scowled back at her.

I should go back out there and apologize, she thought. But her feet remained firmly planted.

She didn't want to face him right now. She didn't want to face anyone. The weird, heavy feeling in her stomach was just too hard to ignore.

All Jessica knew was she had to get out of the Riot before she embarrassed herself—and Evan—any more.

Jessica Wakefield

I've pretty much always been surrounded by guys. I know it sounds obnoxious, but it's just true. Ken, Christian, Sam, Bruce, Aaron, Todd . . . Okay, but that's another story.

It wasn't until this year that guys started to thoroughly confuse me. I mean it was Will, then Jeremy, then Will, but still Jeremy, then definitely Will. Will. Will.

But it's not like I haven't really liked guys before. I've even been in love before. And I've always been able to just pick up the pieces, put on a smile, and move on to the next lucky guy. (Or the next victim, depending on how you look at it.)

So why not now? Is it really the way Evan looks? If I picked another guy, would I feel differently — less tense and confused?

Maybe Elizabeth has been right all along. Maybe the idea is just to find a guy who thinks of nothing but you and then have a boring, solid relationship.

At least when she was with Todd, she was never this confused.

SHOULD HAVE KNOWN BETTER

Jessica's eyes blinked open as she heard a rapping on her bedroom door.

Please, oh please, let it be Mom, she begged silently. *Please don't let it be . . .*

"Jessica? Can I come in?" Elizabeth. Of course.

Jessica stifled a groan at the sound of her sister's voice. "Sure," she replied, pushing her snarled hair back from her face.

Elizabeth practically tiptoed into the room and carefully shut the door behind her.

"You're still in your nightgown," she observed.

"Yeah. I don't feel all that well today," Jessica said, rolling over onto her side.

"Oh, *really?*" Elizabeth said, as if divining special meaning from Jessica's comment. "That might answer my question for me."

"Which question is that?" Jessica asked. She would have looked at Elizabeth, but her eyes felt like lead balls and she had a feeling she didn't want to see her sister's expression anyway.

Elizabeth pushed a huge pile of clothes off

Jessica's desk chair and sat down, bringing her face to Jessica's eye level. So much for avoidance. "Why did you ditch Evan last night?"

Was it just Jessica, or had Elizabeth grown more direct since she'd started hanging out with Conner?

Jessica looked down at her sheets and slowly exhaled. She'd been over this about a trillion times, and she always came to the same, staggeringly astute conclusion. "I don't know."

"You don't know," Elizabeth repeated.

Jessica groaned and flipped over onto her back, pushing both hands into her hair. "I really don't know," she said, her voice rising to a high, feeble pitch. "I mean, I was so tense. It was like I didn't even want to be there. I didn't know what to say or do. And I kept thinking about Will. And then I saw Lila and Cherie watching me, and I—"

"Were you . . ." Elizabeth paused as if unable to comprehend what she was about to say. "Were you *ashamed* of being seen with Evan?"

"No! I—"

"Because of his hair? Because of the way he dresses?" Elizabeth was standing now. "Jessica, you have to be—"

"It wasn't that!" Jessica blurted out, sitting up. For no apparent reason, tears sprang to her eyes. "I *like* Evan . . . sort of. And you know I've never had any problem dancing with people I *don't* even like. But when he pulled me close last night, it felt so . . .

126

wrong." She exhaled heavily and hugged her knees to her chest. "I know it sounds shallow, but I don't know. I can't think of any other reason for being so uncomfortable. Maybe I am just an image-conscious freak."

Elizabeth's forehead was crisscrossed with lines, as if she were contemplating an SAT word problem. "Jess, maybe you're just not over Will. I mean, maybe that's why you didn't want to be with Evan."

"Of course I'm not over Will," Jessica said. "We just broke up. But does that mean I'm going to feel physically ill every time I try to dance with somebody?"

"It doesn't sound like you," Elizabeth said.

"I know!" Jessica exclaimed. "That's what's so weird."

Elizabeth took a deep breath and let it out slowly. Jessica studied her sister's face, and her stomach turned. There was disappointment there, and Jessica knew what that meant. Elizabeth did think Jessica was shallow. She did think this was all about the hair and the clothes.

Jessica felt her face start to redden with indignation. She was sick of Elizabeth playing the behavioral police.

"Well, whatever the reason was, I really think you should apologize to Evan," Elizabeth said finally.

"And I really think you should mind your own business," Jessica snapped.

Elizabeth blanched. "Fine," she said. "Then I will." She turned and stalked out of the room, slamming the door behind her.

"And the high-and-mighty has spoken," Jessica muttered, trying to maintain her level of anger. Unfortunately she couldn't ignore the hollow pit in her stomach. Jessica bent forward, touching her forehead to her knees.

She wished she knew why she was so confused. She wished she hadn't let Elizabeth come in here in the first place. She wished she had locked her door and slept till noon. She wished Elizabeth had never gotten the job with Sedona so they would have never mentioned having a celebration so she wouldn't be in the mess she was in now.

But most of all, for about the three-millionth time in her life, Jessica wished her sister wasn't so *right*.

She was going to have to talk to Evan.

"Yes! Strike one!" Tia raised her fist into the air.

"Uh . . . Tia?" Trent tapped her on the shoulder. "This is bowling. You don't call out 'strike one' when you knock all the pins down."

"So?" she asked, reaching up to tighten her long ponytail. "It was a strike. And it was the first one I've made the whole game. Strike one." She smiled and held her index finger in front of his face. "Besides, I gotta yell something. I gotta show some attitude in my cool new bowling shirt."

Tia held out her arms to properly display the huge, teal button-down she'd bought at a thrift store that morning. The name Buzz was embroidered over the left breast pocket, and the back read Lou's Lumber in big, black letters.

"I like a girl with fashion sense." Trent walked over to the ball return and picked up a shiny, black ball. "So you want to see attitude? I'll show you attitude." He grinned smugly and stepped up to the white line. A second later the ball crashed into the pins, sending all of them flying. "Oh, yeah! That's right! Ten pins go *down!*" He knelt down and made a slicing motion with his arm.

Tia shook her head, laughing. When Trent first suggested they go bowling, she'd hesitated. She had never been very good at the game, and she was afraid she'd make a total fool out of herself. But there was no competition here. Trent was out for fun only.

When she'd let go of the ball too late and it had ended up bouncing down the lane, Trent had clapped her on the back and said, "Excellent dribble!"

Angel probably would have spent fifteen minutes instructing her on her technique and making her feel like an idiot—inadvertently, of course.

It was nice to be out with Trent. In fact, it was nice to be out with any guy after hanging out with so many paired-off friends over the last few days. It wasn't just Conner anymore; it was Elizabeth-and-Conner. And Ken-and-Maria. And Jessica-and-Evan—or whatever guy she had her sights on at the moment. And now Andy-and-Six?

This was the first time in a long while that Tia was on the lonely side of the couple line. And she didn't like it.

Plus here it was Saturday, and she still hadn't heard back from Angel. If it weren't for Trent, she'd probably be at home, sobbing her eyes out and imagining all sorts of awful things—like Angel realizing she was just too young and uncool for him now that he was in college or Angel meeting some gorgeous, seductive coed and becoming hypnotized by her.

Besides, bowling wasn't *really* a date. Her *grandfather* took her bowling.

"You know, all this attitude is making me hungry," Trent said, patting his stomach. "What do you say we blow off the rest of this game and go get some food?"

Tia raised her eyebrows. "Are you really hungry? Or are you scared that I'm on a roll now and might catch up?"

"Catch up?" he repeated, chuckling. "You're, like, seventy-four points behind."

"Okay, okay," she said, rolling her eyes. "I guess I could go for a diet Coke."

They headed down to the other side of the bowling alley toward the fluorescent-lit snack bar. Trent studied the list of items on the marquee sign behind the counter.

A miserable-looking kid in a paper hat leaned toward them. "Good afternoon," he said somberly. "What can I get you?"

Trent stole a quick glance at Tia and grinned, obviously sizing her up. "Let's see. . . . We'll take one diet Coke, one regular Coke, two orders of nachos, two hot dogs, and a basket of Tater Tots."

"Trent!" Tia shouted. "Do I *look* like I eat that much?"

"Oh, I'm sorry. Good point," he said, staring at the food guy with a serious expression. "Better make that *two* orders of Tater Tots."

Tia whacked Trent on the shoulder but couldn't wipe the grin from her face.

"Okay. Whatever," the kid mumbled. He disappeared into the kitchen area.

"What are you doing? I just wanted a drink," Tia said, even as her stomach grumbled.

"Hey, it's way past my feeding time," Trent answered, patting his flat tummy. "C'mon, don't make me eat alone. Let me buy you some lunch."

"But . . ."

Food could be considered a date, she thought.

"That stuff is so fattening," she said. As if she cared. Her metabolism worked faster than Andy's mouth moved.

"Come on, girl," Trent teased, reaching out and shaking her long, brown ponytail. "You gotta live a little." He pulled out his wallet and started counting out a few bills.

"Okay, but you're *not* paying," Tia said, grabbing his wrist. *Paying for food is* definitely *a date.*

"Here you go," the guy in the cap announced, pushing a tray toward Trent. "That'll be $15.42."

Before Tia had even touched her purse, Trent slapped a twenty into the kid's hand. "Keep the change," he said as Tia fumbled with her wallet. She managed to extract a wrinkled five-dollar bill, but Trent snapped it out of her fingers and stuffed it back into her open purse. "Too late," he said, picking up the tray. "But I *will* let you select the table."

Tia sighed and headed for a booth. "Okay," she said, settling onto the hard, orange Formica bench. "But next time I pay."

Then she stopped breathing.

Had she just said "next time"?

Apparently she had because Trent was grinning hugely as he munched on a nacho. "Excellent," he said.

Yeah, Tia thought, every trace of appetite completely extinguished. *Excellent.*

Andy pulled his mom's minivan to a stop in front of a yellow brick building. The dark green wooden sign above the door read Hanson's Sporting Goods in white block letters. Three faceless mannequins stood in various athletic poses in the front display windows. One was ready to putt a golf ball, another held a fishing pole, and the third wore a blue Speedo swimsuit and carried a volley-ball.

Groaning, Andy tapped his fingers on the steering wheel. He couldn't see himself doing any of those things.

"Well, might as well get this over with," he muttered, stepping out of the car. He was just going to have to try not to talk because if he did, he'd definitely expose his monumental ignorance of all things athletic.

Once inside, Andy immediately recognized the crisp, earthy smell of new clothes—the same smell Six always had about her.

"Hey!" Six's eardrum-rupturing greeting emanated from the back of the store.

As Andy's eyes slowly adjusted to the indoor lights, he could see Six bounding up to him, her ever-present ponytail flying.

"I was just wondering if you were going to show up," she said. "I mean, it's way too beautiful out to be inside shopping, but I'm glad you came."

Andy didn't bother to mention that if he wasn't there, he'd probably be in his room with the curtains drawn, playing Rogue Squadron.

"Me too," he said.

Six lifted her arm and leaned against a shelf full of tennis balls.

"So, I had a really great time last night," she said, smiling up at him.

Andy's palms started to sweat. Uh-oh. *Here we go,* Andy thought. She was going to ask when they could do it again. If he wanted to be exclusive. What color he wanted to paint the baby's room.

"You did?" he asked, looking around for an escape route. She was smiling kind of flirtatiously. And her eyes seemed to be sparkling a tad too much. But that might have been a reflection of all the fluorescent lights in the store.

"Yeah!" Six exclaimed. "Your friends are *sooo* cool! Thanks so much for including me."

Andy allowed himself to exhale. "Hey, no problem. I know everyone really liked you."

"You think so?" Six asked, standing up straight.

"I know so," Andy answered, amused. His pulse started to slow a bit. She was wearing one of those grins that she couldn't wipe off if she tried. Forget Elizabeth. He was right. Six was just psyched to be hanging out with seniors.

Andy clapped and looked around at the rows and rows of clothing racks. "So, where do we start? I'm ready for the transformation into Andrew Marsden, Mountain Man."

"That could take a while," Six said, rolling her eyes at him and grabbing his wrist. "But I love a challenge," she said.

As she pulled him to the back of the store, Andy couldn't help laughing. As long as she didn't love *him,* she could dress him however she wanted.

<u>Andy's List of Things</u>
to <u>Pack</u> for the <u>Big</u> <u>Hike</u>

1. Sunscreen
2. Sunglasses
3. Insect repellent
4. Flashlight
5. Swiss Army pocketknife (in case I get chased by a mountain lion or something. Plus you never know when you'll need a Phillips-head screwdriver.)
6. First-aid kit (in case pocketknife fails when I get chased by a mountain lion)
7. Compass
8. Map (in case compass fails)
9. Cellular phone (in case map fails)
10. Canteen of Dr Pepper
11. Doritos
12. Sony Discman
13. My last will and testament (in case everything above fails)

Honey, I'm Home

"Man, didn't you just love that kung fu scene at the end?" Trent said as he pulled up in front of Tia's house. "I couldn't believe the special effects. I thought I was gonna choke on my Milk Duds!"

"I know!" Tia exclaimed. "It was unbelievable. Definitely blew *The Matrix* out of the water."

Trent killed the engine and turned to Tia. "It's so cool that you like action movies. I've never met a girl who would choose Jackie Chan over Sandra Bullock."

Laughing, Tia unhooked her seat belt. "Please. I haven't seen a Sandra Bullock movie since *Speed*."

Trent laughed again, but as it faded into a small chuckle, Tia caught that look coming over his face. That I'm-gonna-kiss-you look. Her heart started to pound, and she realized that she definitely wouldn't mind if he went for it.

And that thought upset her to the point of nausea.

This is wrong, she reminded herself. *You've got to be straight with the guy before things get out of hand. Again.*

"You know, I had a really great time," he said, his voice low.

"Me too," she replied, trying not to meet his gaze. She did have a good time. A fantastic time, in fact. But it had to stop here.

"Maybe we could do this again soon," he said, inching ever so slightly toward her.

"Maybe," she replied. *Don't look at him,* she commanded herself. If her lips weren't facing his, he wouldn't have a clear target and maybe she could get out of this unscathed.

"Tia?"

She glanced up. *Damn!* Why couldn't she control her knee-jerk reactions? Once she was looking into his warm, brown eyes, she couldn't seem to get herself to look away.

Get out! Don't do this! she shouted inwardly. But she couldn't move. Maybe he was somehow hypnotizing her. Or maybe all that fat-laden food she'd eaten was weighing her down. In any case, she had temporarily lost control of her muscles.

"I know this sounds like a line," he said in that deep, chill-inducing voice. "But you're really beautiful." His eyes started to close, and he inched even closer.

Tia caught a sudden whiff of his spicy cologne and the breath mint he'd popped after the movie.

Okay, maybe just one little kiss . . .

But just as Tia was about to let her eyes slip

closed, she glimpsed a tiny bit of blue over his left shoulder—something that immediately flooded her with icy-cold fear.

"Oh my God!" she exclaimed, pulling back.

There, in her parents' driveway, was Angel's car.

"What? What's wrong?" Trent sat up straight again, his eyes wide with worry.

"Uh . . . nothing," she said, grasping for the door handle. "I—I just remembered something I forgot to do. I'm sorry, but I've really got to go."

Tia quickly hopped out of the car, slammed the door, and raced across the front lawn, Trent and his feelings almost completely forgotten. Her heart pounded against her rib cage like an animal trying to escape a trap. What if Angel saw her? What if he was looking out the window this very minute?

She burst through the front door, gasping for breath, even though she'd only run about five yards.

"Hey, there you are." Angel sat on the living-room floor, playing Nintendo with Miguel and Tomás. He looked amazing. He looked better than Tia ever remembered him looking before.

He looked like the guy she was supposed to love.

"H-Hey," she said.

"What's wrong?" Angel asked, standing up. Of course he knew something was wrong. He could probably tell from her face that she was about to get kissed five seconds ago. He knew her too well to—

"Don't I get a hug?" Angel asked, opening his arms.

Tia fell into his arms, feeling like a guilty criminal about to be handed her verdict. "God, I missed you," she said, her eyes closed tightly as he wrapped his arms around her.

"Come on," she heard Miguel say. "Let's go to our room before these guys go all kissy."

The muffled noise of an engine starting sounded from the street. Out of the corner of her eye Tia could see Trent's car gradually disappear down the block. She sighed in relief, her pulse finally slowing to normal levels, grateful that Trent hadn't followed her inside after she went psycho on him.

"Surprised?" Angel asked, pulling back slightly.

"You have no idea," Tia answered.

"There's something I've been wanting to do for days," Angel said, lacing his fingers through hers as he led her over to the couch.

What's that? Tia thought. *Answer my e-mails? Return my calls?* Then she gave herself a mental slap. *She* was the one who had just gotten back from a date with someone else. Angel was the one who had just driven over five hours to see her.

Tia plopped down onto the couch, and before Angel's butt had even hit the cushion, his mouth was on hers. Surprised, it took Tia a second to adjust herself so that she could get her arms around him. Angel hadn't kissed her this passionately in ages.

When he finally broke away, his eyes were a little glassy and Tia was grinning stupidly.

I guess absence really does make the heart grow fonder, she thought as he leaned in to kiss her again.

So what the heck is wrong with me?

Jessica lay sprawled across her bedspread, one hand supporting her chin, the other absently turning pages in a book called *Legends of the Silver Screen.* Each spread featured a black-and-white photo of a renowned Hollywood actor or actress, along with a brief biography. Maria had brought it to theater class the day before, and Jessica had begged her to let her borrow it.

So far she'd found the book extremely informative. For the past five minutes she'd been flipping back and forth between page twenty-three and page forty-four, trying to decide who she would rather make out with on-screen—James Dean or a young Cary Grant.

Cary Grant had those dark, classically handsome features and a sweet, playful smile. And he had a nice body. Definitely the type of guy who could sweep you off your feet and carry you off Tarzan style. But James Dean's brooding eyes and that alluring pout oozed sexuality in a rebellious, bad-boy way.

Of course, it didn't really matter which one she picked. Both guys were gone now anyway. And even if they had survived this long, they'd be unrecognizably older.

Jessica sighed and continued breezing through the book. She turned another page, and a stunning face stared back at her. Blond. Perfectly symmetrical features. Heart-shaped face. Kittenish eyes. A flawlessly constructed slope of a nose . . . Grace Kelly.

If I could look like anyone, Jessica thought, tracing the photo with her finger, *she'd be my top pick.*

On the opposite page was another, smaller photo of Grace Kelly taken during her wedding to Prince Rainier of Monaco. Underneath, the caption read, "The princess of American cinema becomes true royalty. . . ."

Jessica studied the picture. Grace Kelly in her white dress and sparkling tiara certainly looked every bit the part of a fairy-tale princess. But next to her, in his formal military dress, Prince Rainier seemed more like . . . well . . . like an elegant toad than a storybook prince. How could someone that beautiful fall for a short, squat guy with a pug face?

Of course, he was a *prince.* And he probably had other good qualities, deep down where it truly counted. But Jessica still couldn't quite process the image of the two of them standing side by side. It just seemed wrong on some level—like a clashing outfit or a pair of mismatched shoes.

"Jessica, honey?" Her mother's head suddenly

poked through the doorway. "The phone is for you. Didn't you hear it?"

"No, Mom. Sorry," Jessica replied. "I turned the ringer off so I could . . . um . . . nap." No sense trying to explain to her mother that she was being purposefully antisocial. After the old "go-out-and-have-fun" therapy exploded in her face, she figured a few days of seclusion would probably be easier—and safer.

"I see. Well, there's someone named Evan on the line."

Jessica's stomach turned, and she actually flinched. He must have been calling her to tell her off for what she'd done. He probably had *a lot* to say on the subject.

"Mom? Could you tell him I'm not here?" Jessica asked, her sweaty fingers still clutching the book. "Please?"

"Jessica," her mother said in a disapproving tone.

"Look, I can't explain it right now," Jessica said, hoping to head her off. "It's all a big, huge mess that I'm planning on fixing, but I just need more time."

"All right." Her mother shook her head. "But just this once." She turned and walked out of the room, shutting the door behind her.

Jessica felt her entire body slacken with relief. She'd dodged the bullet for now, but she knew she was going to have to talk to Evan sometime.

She looked down at Grace Kelly's wedding

picture again and sighed. "You obviously knew something I don't."

Tia picked up her fork and swirled it around in her penne, rearranging it on her plate so it appeared to be disappearing. She smiled tentatively at Angel and hoped he didn't notice she was behaving like a little kid who didn't want to eat her vegetables instead of a girl on a date at an Italian restaurant.

She wasn't sure how much longer she could pretend to be eating. What made her think she could go through with this? With every morsel she swallowed, her stomach seemed to be expanding dangerously. Soon she would reach critical mass and explode all over the place.

Why'd she have to eat all those greasy snacks earlier? Why'd she even go out with Trent in the first place? And why the heck didn't Angel call and warn her he'd be coming? Did he just take it for granted she'd have nothing better to do than wait around the house on a Saturday?

She glanced back up at him, watching his face rather than actually listening to him talk. It had only been a few weeks since he'd gone off to Stanford, but somehow it seemed longer—as if she hadn't set eyes on him for months.

". . . so it's already ten till the hour, but this professor keeps on talking and talking," Angel was saying, waving his fork in tiny circles. "A few people get up to head out to their other classes, and he yells at them to sit back down. So we just sat there taking notes, too scared to move. Finally about fifteen minutes later he realizes it and lets us go. I was ten minutes late for work, but as soon as I explained that I'd been trapped in Dr. Eisner's class, my manager completely understood." He laughed and shook his head, his large, dark eyes twinkling in the candlelight.

God, she'd missed that. She'd missed *him*.

What was wrong with her anyway? Her boyfriend was finally here, and all she could do was mope and obsess about food.

Tia glanced around, suddenly aware of the total silence at their table. She had no idea when Angel had stopped talking. Or how long she'd sat there, nodding along to nothing.

"So . . . ," she said hurriedly. "College doesn't sound *too* bad. Even though it keeps you totally swamped all the time." Her voice came out sounding somewhat sour and resentful, which she totally hadn't intended.

Angel looked down at his spaghetti and shrugged. "Yeah, well . . . I guess it could be worse. But you're right about it keeping me busy. You wouldn't believe how crazy I've been!" He took a sip of water and grinned. "Which is why I haven't had time to answer your millions of messages," he said teasingly.

Tia's eyes narrowed, and her fork dropped to her

plate with a loud clang. "*Millions* of messages?" she repeated in a hissing whisper. "I haven't sent you *millions* of messages."

"I know," he said, his eyes wide with surprise. "I just—"

"What?" Tia asked, her body temperature rising. "So just because I actually take the time to call or write now and then makes me some clingy little girl? Is that it?"

"No." Angel grabbed her hand, but Tia pulled it away. "Tia, that's not what I—"

"I mean, forgive me for interrupting your precious study time," she railed on. "God forbid you actually take one minute to type a few lines of e-mail and press send!"

"I did write back," Angel snapped.

"Yeah, *once*," Tia shot back. "It must have taken you a whole minute to compose that work of art."

Angel's face went flat. His lips pursed, and he gripped the sides of the table. Tia instinctively knew that he was waiting for her to calm down so he could try to reason with her. He always knew when she just needed time to vent.

A wave of remorse washed over Tia. For the last couple of weeks she'd been so afraid of losing Angel, and now that they were together, she was practically pushing him away.

"God, I'm sorry," she said, closing her eyes and pressing her fingertips against her lids. "I didn't mean to make a scene. I know you're insanely busy at school. And I understand that. Really. I just . . . I don't know."

Angel let out a long, weary sigh. "It's okay. You're right." Angel released the table and rubbed his hand over his face. He looked so tired and so sad. Tia's heart responded with a pang. He must have been exhausted from the drive, and he'd still found the energy to get all dressed up and take her out. How ungrateful could she be?

"Things are just crazed right now, Tee," Angel said slowly. "But as soon as they slow down, I swear I—"

"We can talk about this some other time," Tia interrupted. She reached out and took the hand she'd rejected moments before. "Let's just forget about it, okay? At least for tonight."

Angel smiled and lifted her hand to his mouth, kissing it gently. Tia felt a new warmth spread over her skin. One that had nothing to do with anger.

And I'm going to forget about Trent, she told herself. *Forever.*

Angel Desmond

In computer class the other day Professor Eisner talked on and on about something called competing systems. This is when one program has to be completely shut down in order for another one to work.

It made me think. That's sort of how I've been feeling lately.

You see, I love Tia. I really do. But when I'm at Stanford, it's like I can't find a place for her, like I can't function there if I get focused on her.

And the few times I have called her, my old "Tia" programming kicks in and I become completely useless at school stuff. I can't concentrate. I can't relax. It's as if my whole brain goes haywire.

See? Competing systems.

So what do I do? I can't completely shut down either part of my life. And I can't choose between them.

I have to figure out something soon. Otherwise I have the uneasy feeling I'm headed for a total systems crash.

Say What?

Tia had to talk to someone. And fast.

When Angel had kissed her good-bye at the front door, she was completely sure that she was going to call Trent and end it. But then she'd made the mistake of checking the answering machine.

Trent had left her an amazingly sweet message, and it had sent her into another fit of confusion. She'd had a great time with Trent that day. She'd had a miserable time with Angel that night. Angel was leaving. Trent was here. What was she supposed to do? Forgo the possibility of an enjoyable, healthy relationship so she could hang on to a long-distance one just because she felt like she should?

Tia groaned and fell face first onto her bed. No. That wasn't it. It wasn't like she felt she *should* be with Angel. She loved him. Didn't she?

"Okay, okay, here's what we know," Tia said, flipping over, sitting up, and shaking her hair out of her face. "One, I'm a horrible person. Two, I really like Trent. Three, I really love Angel. And four, I'm going to have a nervous breakdown."

She had to get out of the house.

Grabbing her battered El Carro varsity jacket, Tia rushed out of her room and straight through the back door. She knew exactly who she needed to talk to. Luckily he was only a shortcut away.

By the time she was rapping on Conner's kitchen door, Tia already felt better. Conner would definitely help her sort this out. And with his blunt manner it would take about two-point-five seconds.

"Tia? What are you doing here?" Conner asked, opening the door. His hair stuck up on one side, and his shirt was all rumpled. Tia wondered if he'd actually already hit the sheets. By nine o'clock?

"Conner. I'm so glad you're here," she exclaimed, pushing past him and walking through the kitchen and into the living room. "I've got a major problem and—"

Tia stopped short. Elizabeth was sitting on the couch, her clothes and hair in a similar state of disarray to Conner's.

Oops.

"Hi, Tia," Elizabeth said, smiling politely as she straightened her shirt.

"Hey, there," Tia replied with an empty grin. Did these two ever spend any time apart anymore?

Don't be a jerk, Tia told herself. *It's Saturday night.* And she supposed it wasn't Elizabeth's fault—or Conner's—that they were so incredibly, sickeningly happy.

"Uh, look. Never mind," Tia said, changing her course and stepping backward into the kitchen. "Forget I was here. You just go back to . . . to doing what you were doing."

"Okay," Conner said, walking past her and sitting down on the couch.

"Conner!" Elizabeth exclaimed, shoving his shoulder.

He rolled his eyes and rubbed his shoulder with his hand. "You don't have to get violent," he said. Then he sighed. "Come on in, Tee."

"Don't do me any favors," Tia said moodily. Part of her just wanted to bolt through the kitchen and teach Conner a lesson by never talking to him again. But she really needed this advice. And two heads were probably better than one anyway. Tia trudged into the living room and flung herself into the big, comfy armchair.

"Angel came into town to see me," she said, looking over at them. "He was at my house when I got back." She paused briefly. "After being out with Trent all day."

Conner closed his eyes. "I thought you told me you were going to be straight with Angel," he said.

"I was!" Tia said, leaning forward. "But then—"

"But then you weren't," Conner said.

Tia clasped her hands together, trying to fight back a wave of anger. Why wouldn't he even listen to

153

her? And why was Elizabeth just sort of staring off into space?

"He's the one who never returned my phone calls," Tia reminded him. "I can't exactly talk to him if he won't even get in touch with me."

Conner rolled his eyes. "Well, he's here now. And you have to talk to him. That's all I'm going to say to you."

Tia stood up. "Since when are you so moralistic, Mr. Flavor of the Week?" she asked, noting the immediate blush that rose to Elizabeth's cheeks. The girl was paying attention now. "Name one girl you *haven't* cheated on."

A thick silence fell over the room. Conner slowly stood up, his six-foot-tall frame dwarfing Tia's. "Go," he said, staring at her with an angry expression she'd seen before, but never trained on her.

"Conner—," Tia and Elizabeth both said at the same time.

"I'll call you tomorrow, Tee," Conner said stonily. "Right now I really think you should leave. Go home and call your boyfriend."

Tia turned on her heel and walked shakily through the kitchen, her heart sagging. This was totally humiliating. Conner was her best friend. He never spoke to her like that in front of anyone. And he never put anything, even making out with a girl, in front of her. And she'd never felt compelled to speak to him that way either. What was wrong with her? It was like she was possessed.

As she opened the door, Tia heard someone behind her and froze.

"Tia? Are you okay?"

It was Elizabeth.

Tia turned slowly but could barely meet her friend's eye. "Yeah. I'm sorry about what I just said."

Elizabeth shrugged and forced a smile. "It's okay. I mean, it's probably true." She let out a tense laugh. "I mean, up until now . . ."

"He hasn't cheated on you, Liz," Tia said. "Don't worry."

Letting out a little sigh, Elizabeth visibly relaxed. "So what are you going to do about Angel?"

"I don't know," Tia said, swinging open the door. "But I'll figure it out."

Before Elizabeth could say anything more or lecture her on her moral responsibility to Angel, Tia was out the door.

Andy shifted the weight of his backpack and continued up the craggy hill. What started out as a gentle, grassy slope had become steeper and more treacherous in the last half mile. And judging from the jutting boulders of the skyline up ahead, it was only going to get worse.

Still, he had to admit it was beautiful. Since they'd first started the hike, the sky had gone from a grayish lavender to a soft pink and now a deep, vibrant blue.

He hadn't gotten up this early since . . . well, maybe he'd never gotten up this early before—especially on a weekend. But after seeing the sun rise behind the hills, he could definitely understand the appeal.

An explosion of familiar laughter suddenly drowned out the chirping of birds. Andy looked farther up the line of hikers and spotted Six's braids bouncing merrily across her back. When he'd arrived at the starting-off point that morning, she'd greeted him cheerfully, but after that, they'd barely spoken. Not exactly typical behavior of a love-struck female specimen. He was in the clear.

Of course, considering her uphill speed was twice as fast as his (even with a more loaded-down backpack), it would have been tough for them to walk and talk together. He could see how regular workouts like this might have developed her amazing lung power.

"How are you doing back here?" Travis Hanson's hulking frame stood in front of him, blocking out the sunlight. The guy must have broken from the front of the line and waited for him. Andy felt a pang of insulted pride.

"Great. Doing just great," Andy replied, trying to quicken his pace for effect.

"It's nice out here. Isn't it?" Travis asked, falling into step beside Andy.

"Yep. Sure is." Andy was amazed at Travis's effortless

speech. His own voice was coming out weak and breathless. He inhaled deeply and added, "Wish we could get school credit for this. It definitely beats being locked in a stuffy classroom all day."

"No doubt," Travis said. "That's why I'll be doing nothing but this for a whole year after graduation."

Andy stopped in his tracks. "What? You mean you aren't going to college?" It shocked him to think Travis might not be the academic type—especially since his father was a professor.

"Oh no. I'm definitely going," Travis said, laughing. "But I'm going to take a year off before I start and do some traveling. A buddy and I are going to hike and bicycle through Europe. I figure it'll be a really cool experience. Plus then I won't be so burned out on school when I start college."

Andy nodded silently. His mind whirled as they resumed their easy pace up the mountain. A year off? Doing nothing but traveling? That did sound pretty incredible. Maybe Travis was onto something. If he could do it, maybe Andy didn't have to start college right away either.

Just thinking there might be other options for his future made Andy feel better. Lighter, even—as if his weighty backpack had magically emptied itself.

"So tell me more about this year-off thing," he said, glancing at Travis. "It's something I might want to look into."

* * *

Angel strolled through the front door of House of Java and was immediately surrounded by the smells of fresh espresso and soft jazz music in the background.

A sense of comfort enfolded him like a blanket. There were times at Stanford when his head hurt from studying and his heart hurt from homesickness, and all he'd have to do was close his eyes and remember this coffeehouse in order to feel better.

He and Tia used to come here all the time. Especially on Sunday mornings—like now. They'd each order a latte and laugh about everything that happened over the weekend. He'd thought about stopping by Tia's house and asking her to join him, but she'd been feeling ill when he dropped her off the night before, so he'd decided to let her sleep in. Instead he was planning on bringing her coffee in bed.

It squeezed his heart to think about how she'd made it through their dinner date even when she felt so ill. All for his sake. Here he had this incredible, devoted girlfriend, and he couldn't even bother to spend a little time on an e-mail or two. What a jerk he was.

What had happened to them? He had been really looking forward to seeing Tia, but when he'd finally gotten her alone, everything had felt weird. Everything he'd said had come out awkwardly—as if they hadn't seen each other in months instead of weeks. Things had never been that tense between them.

"Hey, Angel!" Jeremy Aames smiled at him from behind the counter. "What's up? You back for a visit or something?"

"Yeah. Kind of a last-minute thing," Angel said, returning the grin. "So how goes football? Big Mesa still stomping everyone's butts?"

Jeremy shrugged. "We beat Seneca Heights last night. So far it's a winning season. But I'm too superstitious to get all cocky yet."

"Yeah, I hear you," Angel said, chuckling as he scanned the menu board.

"Listen, man." Jeremy's voice lowered to a somber pitch. "I'm sorry about you and Tia."

Angel's eyebrows flew up as his heart gave an ominous thud. "Me and Tia?" he asked.

"Uh . . . yeah. You know." Jeremy frowned in confusion.

"No." Angel rolled his shoulders back defensively. "What?"

Jeremy stood up straight, and his face suddenly became unnaturally pinched. He busied himself with the cappuccino maker. "Nothing," he said.

An uneasy chill shot through Angel, and he pressed his palms into the counter. "Tell me what's going on," he said in his most threatening tone. He'd never touch Jeremy, but it also never hurt to be able to make someone cut to the chase.

Jeremy sighed and dropped his head forward. Then he looked Angel right in the eye and walked over so that he was standing directly in front of him. "She's seeing someone else, man," Jeremy said, causing Angel's heart to wither and die just like that. "I just figured you guys had broken up."

"What?" Angel yelled so loudly that the entire café turned to stare. "You're not serious," he said, only a bit more quietly.

Jeremy just stared at him with an uncomfortable yet pitying look on his face.

A strange, numbing sensation crept over Angel's body.

Realization plowed through him like a steamroller, making him doubt everything he trusted. Tia had been acting kind of strange yesterday. Distant— almost cold. Except, of course, when she was yelling at him. Slowly, distractedly, Angel backed away from the counter.

"I'm really sorry, man," Jeremy said, picking up a dirty cup someone had left on the counter. "I shouldn't have been the one to tell you."

"Don't worry about it," Angel mumbled, turning toward the front door. He could barely see straight. "I've got to go."

Jeremy Aames

Back at the beginning of the year, I wanted to kill Melissa Fox.

Okay, I didn't even know her, but she was the one who told me about Jessica and Will, so I hated her by association. It was the whole "kill-the-messenger" thing, I guess.

I just hope Angel doesn't feel the same way about me right now. Because he's kind of a huge guy. And I kind of don't want to be hospitalized.

Tia lay sprawled across the living-room couch, staring blankly at the ceiling. The rest of the family was off at a Little League picnic, but she'd begged to stay behind, explaining that she didn't feel well.

For once in her life, the house was quiet, but Tia wasn't even capable of enjoying it. The voices in her head were too loud.

Okay. So she'd made a mistake. She shouldn't have messed around with Trent, and she shouldn't have continued to hang out with him. But why did everyone have to rub that in her face? They had no idea what it had been like for her—not being able to see Angel, him being too busy to call or write. It made her unable to think clearly.

All she knew for sure was that she didn't want anyone to get hurt.

The doorbell suddenly rang, making her jump upright. It was Angel. It had to be.

Okay, don't screw this up, Tia told herself as she approached the door. All she had to do was play the happy girlfriend for a few more hours. Then Angel would be on his way back to Stanford, and she'd have more time to herself to sort this whole thing through.

Nothing like a healthy dose of avoidance, Tia chided herself.

She fixed a cheerful expression to her face and headed toward the entry. "Hey!" she greeted, pushing the door wide open.

What she saw made the blood halt in her veins. Trent was slouched against one of the porch columns, wearing a drool-worthy, clingy black T-shirt, grinning at her.

"Trent!" she exclaimed, walking onto the front stoop and shutting the door behind her. There was no way she could invite him in—it would prevent her from getting rid of him as quickly as possible. "What are you doing here?"

"Surprised?" he asked. "I was just casually passing by—okay, make that I was purposefully driving to your place—and was wondering if you'd like to grab a late breakfast somewhere."

Tia glanced around, half expecting to find a spy in one of the crepe-myrtle bushes. Standing out in broad daylight with him made her feel incredibly self-conscious.

"I—I can't, Trent. I'm sorry," she stammered. "Things are really hectic today, so if you don't mind . . ." She turned to head back into the house.

"Whoa. Whoa, there." Trent straightened up and

took a couple of steps toward her. "Look, I was just, you know, thinking about yesterday and the fact that I had a lot of fun with you. And I *assumed* you had a good time."

"I had a great time," Tia said with an inadvertent sigh.

"Good," he said. " 'Cause I started to have my doubts after the way you raced off. You know, Tia," he went on, lowering his voice solemnly, "I told you I'd take things slow from now on, and I meant it. If I ever do anything that makes you uncomfortable, just say so. Okay?"

Goose bumps broke out all over Tia's arms as she looked into his warm, very serious eyes. Part of her just wanted to kiss him, and another part wanted to tell him that he was making her uncomfortable right now.

"Listen, Trent. There's something I need to tell you." She took a deep breath, compounding all her courage, and she was about to spill it all out when her heart suddenly leaped into her throat, blocking the words.

Angel's car was pulling into the driveway.

"What the hell is this?" Angel muttered through his clenched teeth.

He slammed the gearshift into park and jumped out of the car, feeling like he could burst right out of his skin.

On the way over to Tia's he'd imagined exactly what he would say.

"*You'll never believe what that Jeremy kid at HOJ told me. . . .*"

And then he would wait for her reaction. He was prepared for her to laugh. He was prepared for her to cry. He was prepared for her to get mad and throw something.

He was *not* prepared to find her eye to eye with some pretty boy dressed up in club gear on a Sunday morning.

Angel slammed the door as hard as he could, announcing his arrival to Baldie, who hadn't noticed him yet. The guy glanced over, seemingly confused. But Tia . . . it tore into his heart to see the guilty, panicked expression on her face. His worst fears were immediately confirmed.

"Angel, wait!" Tia shouted as he crossed the front lawn toward them. "Listen to me. I can explain!"

But her words bounced off him like tennis balls. He couldn't listen. He couldn't even think. All he could do was react.

His fists clenched, his jaw set, and blood pounded through his veins like the beat on a battle drum. No way was he going to let some poser come between him and Tia. He could feel his pulse accelerate as he got closer.

No way.

*   *   *

"Angel!" Tia yelled. "Listen to me! Just *listen!*"

She stepped in front of Trent and held up her hands, her entire body trembling with fear—something she'd thought she would never feel in Angel's presence. But then again, she'd never seen him look this way before either. His eyes were as dark as coal, and a purple-blue vein throbbed down the middle of his forehead. But it was the way he stalked toward them, as if he were an unfeeling mechanism programmed toward a target, that struck her as truly eerie.

"He didn't know about you!" Tia said desperately. "I swear. He didn't know about you!"

That did it. Suddenly, only two steps away from the front steps, Angel seemed to snap out of his trance. Instead of glowering at Trent he shifted his gaze to Tia, his eyes more hurt than murderous.

Trent looked from Tia to Angel and back again, comprehension slowly sweeping over his features. Then he too shot Tia a wounded expression.

So it finally happened. She was surrounded by her worst fears. The guilt was so powerful, Tia could hardly breathe. She had the distinct feeling she was sinking down through the earth.

"What the hell is going on, Tia?" Angel growled.

"Uh, yeah," Trent added awkwardly. "I'd like to know myself."

"Look, I . . . I messed up. I know that," Tia began, her voice trembling along with her body. "I wanted to be straight with you—both of you—but I just didn't know how."

"Aw, man." Trent shook his head at her in obvious disgust, then turned toward Angel. "Look, I'm sorry. I really had no idea she had . . . you know . . . a boyfriend and all."

He gave Tia another look of pure disappointment that sent a knitting needle through her heart. "I'm sorry," she said, hoping for any glimpse of forgiveness. But Trent just turned on his heel and trudged across the yard to his car.

Tia took a deep breath as he drove off. It was just as well. Angel was the person who she really owed an explanation.

She stood silently for a moment, unable to meet Angel's stare. Finally she lifted her gaze, trying to prepare herself for whatever she'd find, but his expression was almost more than she could take. The complete anguish behind his eyes made him seem almost broken. She would have much preferred the scary, angry face to the one he wore now.

Angel slumped against the same post Trent had occupied moments ago. "What the hell do we do now, Tee?" he asked.

His image blurred as hot tears filled her eyes. "I don't know," she whispered. "I don't know anything anymore."

"Come on, Andy! You can do it! Just a few more feet to go!"

Andy grasped the rope with his gloved hands and pulled his body upward, bracing his boots against the steep rock wall. Sweat poured down from his temples into his eyes, nose, mouth. He'd never realized he had so much liquid in him.

Don't look down, he told himself. The last time he'd given in to that temptation he'd lost his foothold and ended up spinning around on the rope like a clumsy trapeze artist.

"Go, Andy, go!" Six cheered from the summit.

Andy focused on her voice and hoisted himself up another foot. *Think up,* he told himself. The sight of the ground several stories below was just too disorienting. It made him think of death—gruesome, organ-splattering death. Instead he'd concentrate on the sky above. Big, fluffy clouds. Cute little birdies. Friendly green aliens in their spaceships. Hey, maybe he could hitch a ride?

"You're almost there! You're doing it, Andy!"

Six's voice, which he'd been able to hear clear down the mountain, suddenly seemed closer than ever. Glancing up, he could see the rounded edge of the summit.

Andy huffed and puffed and yanked his body upward with all his might. Soon Six's brown suede boots came into view. Then her knees. Then the rest of her, bouncing up and down and shouting with joy.

"Yay! You did it!" She grabbed hold of his hand

and pulled him away from the cliff side. "That was so great!"

"Yeah. Yeah, it *was* great," Andy said, sucking in as much oxygen as possible. He unhooked his safety harness and bowed on shaky legs to the other climbers' applause.

"Way to go, Marsden!" Travis called up from his anchoring spot.

Andy felt like Superman. After eighteen years the boldest thing he'd ever done was defeat a virtual alien race with a joystick. Now he could say he'd scaled a towering mountain and laughed death in the face. Well, maybe not death, but at least serious bodily injury.

"Are you hungry?" Six asked. She gestured at some of the other hikers, who were seated along the ground, eating snacks.

"Are you kidding?" he wheezed, taking off his helmet. "I could eat anything. This dirt is looking tasty, even."

Six laughed. "Come on!" she said, grabbing him by the elbow. "Let's find a place to sit."

Andy followed her around the bend of the summit, behind a couple of trees, and over a large boulder to a long, sunny stretch of rock.

She sat down cross-legged and gazed out at the view of the high desert. Andy took off his backpack and sat down beside her, digging in the main pocket for his lunch bag.

"Ah . . ." She sighed, leaning back on her hands. "This is the perfect spot."

"Yeah. It's cool," Andy agreed, reaching in his bag for his packet of Twinkies—Andy's version of trail food.

"I mean, *finally.* At last we can be alone."

"Yeah, fi—" Andy paused as the words penetrated his brain. *Alone?*

He sat there, paralyzed, as Six slowly leaned toward him. He could see the blond tips of her lashes, the flecks of brown in her green eyes, and the constellation of rust-colored freckles spattered across her nose.

And then her mouth met his. Soft and warm, a gentle push of the lips, and then it was over.

Andy's mind felt curiously detached. As if he'd been watching the whole thing instead of actually part of it—even though he'd experienced every sensation. It was like a dream. Or a nightmare. He wasn't sure which.

"See?" she said, her voice lower and sultrier than he'd ever heard it before. "That's much better, don't you think?"

Andy swallowed hard, his packet of Twinkies dropping from his grasp. *Ooookay,* he thought. *What do I do now?*

Tia took a deep breath and ordered herself to look Angel in the eye. She had to tell him the truth.

Now that there was nothing left to lose, all she could do was be honest.

"Angel, I'm sorry," she whispered. "I'm so, so, so sorry."

Angel crossed his arms over his chest, hugging himself. "Just tell me why."

"I just . . . I couldn't handle it," she replied. There were tears in her eyes, and she knew she was just going to have to deal with them. There was no way to avoid crying during this conversation. "You were so . . . gone. I mean, you were off at Stanford and all, but you were also so . . . so *apart* from me. You never wrote back, never answered my calls. I couldn't take being shut out like that."

"But Tee. You don't realize how—"

"I know." Tia held up a hand. "You were totally stressed, I know. Look, I hate it that I've become this clingy little . . . *thing*. You know me. I never thought I'd do that. But I guess I'm just not . . . strong enough or something."

Angel stared down at the concrete steps, his face a mask of lines. She hated seeing him like this. And she was the cause.

"I just miss you so much, Angel," she said softly, reaching out and pulling little leaves from a nearby hedge, one by one. "I don't know what's wrong with me, but I hate the way it feels. It's like I become dysfunctional or something when you're not around."

Angel shoved his fingers into his front pockets. "I

should probably be straight with you too," he said quickly. Tia's heart hit the front step. Had he met somebody too? The thought made her want to pull her insides out through her mouth. But then, she'd done it herself. What kind of person was she?

He shut his eyes and took a deep breath, and Tia prepared herself for the words. "The thing is, I could have called and written you at times. I just . . . didn't. I don't know why."

Tia felt a crumpling sensation inside her. Of course he hadn't fooled around behind her back. Angel, unlike her, was actually a good person.

"I guess it was just easier that way somehow," he went on. "I couldn't handle missing you all the time, so I just didn't deal with it. At all."

His words seemed to tear right through her, but in a way, everything started to make sense. A sad, awful sense.

"And I guess the whole Trent thing was my twisted way of dealing with it," she mumbled shakily.

"I thought things would be better when I came here," he went on. "I thought they could go back to being the same. But . . ."

"It's not," she finished for him.

For a moment no one said anything. She watched as Angel twisted the toe of his tennis shoe against the porch floor. For some reason, she suddenly felt incredibly tired.

"I hate this," she said in a thick voice. "I hate that

you've been gone for, like, two weeks and we just crumbled. I don't get it."

"I know," Angel said, sounding more distant than he had when he was hundreds of miles away at Stanford. "But I can't deal with this, Tia," he continued. "I can't go back to school and worry the whole time about what you're doing. And who with."

Tia's throat swelled. Her eyes stung with fresh tears, and her lips started to tremble. She couldn't believe they were talking this way.

"I know I screwed up," she said, her voice cracking. "But I don't know what to do now. I just don't know what I want anymore."

Angel let out a long sigh. "Maybe we shouldn't do anything. Maybe we should just . . . take a break."

"A break," Tia repeated, staring at his familiar but hardened face and trying desperately not to sob.

"Yeah," he replied, his voice barely a whisper.

Tears raced down Tia's cheeks. Other couples broke up. Other couples took breaks that turned into separations that turned into complete ruin. But not them. They'd always been beyond that. Immune somehow.

But she knew there was nothing she could do right now. She didn't want to feel like this anymore. "Yeah," she heard herself say. "I guess you're right."

They locked eyes for a long, silent moment. Tia sobbed openly, and a few tears streaked down the sides of Angel's face. In a moment of sheer panic Tia considered taking it all back—begging for another chance. But she held back.

"Well, I guess I should get going," Angel said, taking a step down the path.

"Yeah," Tia replied, sniffling. "I guess so."

He reached up and cupped her face in his hands. His palms were cold, and his face looked taut and stretched. He gazed at her for a few seconds, then quickly turned and walked to his car.

Tia wrapped her arms around herself. Leaning back against the front door, she watched as he backed down the driveway, gave her a small wave, and headed down the street.

"Bye, Angel," she whispered.

The car paused at a stop sign, its left blinker flashing. Then it turned and disappeared around the corner.

As soon as it was out of sight, a fierce pain grabbed hold of Tia. She doubled over, sobbing uncontrollably.

It was the second time in a month that she'd sent Angel off to school. But this was different. This good-bye felt like forever.

ELIZABETH WAKEFIELD

12:06 P.M.

Conner just called. Tia and Angel broke up.

Tia and Angel.

You know what this means? It means no one is safe. If it can happen to them, it can happen to anyone.

ANDY MARSDEN

12:22 P.M.

If I tell Six I'm not interested, do you think she'll push me off the side of the mountain and try to make it look like an accident?

JESSICA WAKEFIELD
12:45 P.M.

I'm not shallow. I'm really not. Yes, I admit, there was a time in my life when I was probably the most nondeep person in California, but I honestly think I've changed.

There has to be another reason for this Evan thing, right? I mean, it's not like he asked me to <u>marry</u> him. It was just a dance.

So what's wrong with me?

TIA RAMIREZ

1:47 A.M.

IF YOU LOVE SOMETHING, YOU
SET IT FREE.
IF IT COMES BACK TO YOU, IT
IS YOURS.
IF IT DOES NOT, IT NEVER WAS.

I DID THE RIGHT THING. I DID
THE RIGHT THING.
DID I . . . ?
I DID THE RIGHT THING.